# Dirty Bertie

## A TRIO of TROUBLE

DAVID ROBERTS WRITTEN BY ALAN MACDONALD

**Stripes**

# Collect all the Dirty Bertie books!

# Contents

STRIPES PUBLISHING
An imprint of Magi Publications
1 The Coda Centre, 189 Munster Road,
London SW6 6AW

A paperback original
First published in Great Britain in 2011

ISBN: 978-1-84715-202-2

A CIP catalogue record for this book is available from
the British Library.

Printed and bound in the UK.

10 9 8 7 6 5 4 3 2 1

# Dirty Bertie

## WORMS!

For Christine ~ D R

To the lovely Hylands of Hyland Hall ~ A M

# Contents

# CHAPTER 1

It was Monday morning and Bertie was eating his breakfast.

"Bertie, don't do that!" said his mum, looking up.

"Do what?" said Bertie.

"Let Whiffer lick your spoon. I saw you!"

"He's hungry!" said Bertie.

# Dirty Bertie

"I don't care," sighed Mum. "It's dirty, Bertie."

Bertie inspected his spoon and gave it a lick. It looked clean enough to him.

Just then he heard the post thudding through the letterbox. He jumped down from the table and skidded into the hall. Bertie hardly ever got a letter, but it didn't stop him checking the post. He sorted through the bundle. Dad, Mum, Mum, Dad, boring, boring … wait!

A letter with his name written on it in large wonky letters!

To Bertie

# Dirty Bertie

Bertie burst into the kitchen. "I got a letter!" He tore the envelope open. The decorations on the card could only mean one thing. A party!

Bertie loved birthday parties — he loved the games, the cake and the party bags. Last year he'd had a dog party and everyone had come as a dog. Bertie had been a bloodhound with Dracula fangs. He had wanted dog biscuits for tea but his mum had put her foot down.

Mum picked up the invitation. "Oh lovely, Bertie! Angela's invited you to her party."

"Angela?" said Bertie. The smile drained from his face. "Not Angela Angela?"

"Yes. Angela next door."

# Dirty Bertie

"Bertie's little girlfriend!" teased his sister, Suzy.

Bertie grabbed the invitation and read the message inside.

> please come to my pink
> Birthday party on Friday!
> wear something pink!
> Love and kisses
> from Angela ×××

Bertie's mouth gaped open. His whole body drooped with disappointment. Angela Nicely lived next door and was almost six. She had straight blonde hair, rosy cheeks and large blue eyes. Worst of all she was in love with Bertie. She followed him round like a shadow.

# Dirty Bertie

He didn't want to go to Angela's party, and he definitely didn't want to go to any party where you had to dress in pink. Bertie's favourite colour was brown. Mud was brown, fingernails were brown, poo was brown. Ribbons, bows and ballet shoes, they were pink.

"I don't have to go, do I?" asked Bertie.

"Nose, Bertie," said Mum.

Bertie removed a finger that had strayed up his nose.

"Angela's invited you," said Mum. "How would you feel if you invited Angela and she didn't come?"

"I'd feel glad," said Bertie, truthfully.

"It's a party, Bertie. You love parties," said Mum.

"And you love Angela!" taunted Suzy.

Bertie ignored her. "It'll be terrible. They'll all want to play princesses. Couldn't you say I've got to go to the dentist?"

Mum gave him a look. "That would be a lie, wouldn't it, Bertie?"

"Mum! They'll all be girls," moaned Bertie. "I'll be the only boy!"

"I'm sure it'll be fun. Now, I'm late for work." She kissed him and hurried out. Bertie slumped into a chair.

A pink party with adoring Angela and her friends – could anything be worse?

# CHAPTER 2

The next day Bertie overheard Mrs
Nicely talking to his mum about the
party. It was just as he feared. He was
the only boy invited – along with six of
Angela's friends. "Angela is so excited
about Bertie coming," said Mrs Nicely.
"I think it's so sweet she's invited her
little boyfriend."

# Dirty Bertie

Bertie was nearly sick. Boyfriend? Yuck! He wasn't Angela's boyfriend! If his friends ever heard about the party they'd make fun of him for weeks. He wasn't going and that was final. If his mum wouldn't think of an excuse then he'd have to invent one himself. When it came to cunning plans, Bertie was a master.

In his room he searched under the bed for the shoebox where he kept his top-secret possessions.

# Dirty Bertie

He pulled out a notebook and began to write a list:

**Brilliant** excuses for not going to a party.

1.  A crocodile bit my head off and I'm not talking to anyone.
2.  I have got a rare disease called party-itis which brings me out in terrible spots.
3.  I had baked beans for breakfast, lunch and supper. I think you know what that means.
4.  I have lost my memory.

What party?

# Dirty Bertie

Bertie read back through it. "Brilliant Excuse Number 4" would do the trick. Now all he had to do was talk to Angela and convince her. Then he would be off the hook. No stinky-pinky party for him.

Bertie's chance came on Wednesday lunchtime. He was eating lunch with his friends Darren and Eugene. They were flicking peas at the next table to see if they could land one down the back of Know-All Nick's jumper.

"Hello, Bertie!" said Angela, appearing from nowhere.

Bertie looked at her blankly. "Who are you?" he asked.

Angela giggled. "You are funny, Bertie! Did you get the invitation? You are coming to my party, aren't you?"

Bertie frowned. "Party? What party?"

"Silly! You know, my pink party!"

"PINK Party? Ha ha!" hooted Darren. "Bertie's going to a GIRL'S party!"

Bertie shot him a look. "Sorry, I don't remember any party," he told Angela. "I've lost my memory, you see."

"Gosh!" said Angela. "How?"

"That's just it, I can't remember. I must have got a bang on the head."

"Oh, poor Bertie!" cooed Angela.

Eugene and Darren exchanged glances. "Poor Bertie!" they mimicked.

Angela put her hand on Bertie's. Bertie drew it away quickly.

"Never mind," she said. "The party's at my house on Friday. We're having a bouncy castle."

"Have a nice time," said Bertie, loading more peas on to his spoon.

Angela stamped her foot.

"You've got to come, Bertie. Laura and Maisie are coming. I've told them you're my boyfriend."

# Dirty Bertie

Eugene gurgled and slipped off his chair. Bertie stared hard at Angela as if she looked faintly familiar. "Sorry? What did you say your name was?"

Angela gave a howl of rage and stormed off. Bertie heaved a sigh of relief. It had been a close call but he thought he'd got away with it.

Later that evening Mrs Nicely called to see his mum. Sensing trouble, Bertie hid in his room. But as soon as the front door closed, there was a shout from downstairs.

"BERTIE! Down here! Now!"

Bertie slunk downstairs.

"Right," said Mum. "What's this about losing your memory?"

# Dirty Bertie

Bertie stared at his feet. "Um … yes. It just seems to keep um … going."

"Really? So you don't remember Angela's invitation?"

Bertie knit his brows. "What invitation?" he asked.

Mum folded her arms. "That's a pity, because there's a film you wanted to see at the weekend. I expect you've forgotten that too?"

Bertie hadn't. "Pirates of Blood Island!" he blurted out. He'd been begging to see the film for weeks.

"Ah! So your memory *is* working," said Mum.

"I … um … remember some things. But other things I forget."

"Hmm," said Mum. "Well don't worry because I've marked the party on the

calendar to remind you." She pointed to
Friday the 8th – it was ringed in red.
"And Bertie…"

"Yes?"

"I will not forget."

Bertie slunk out of the kitchen.

He knew when he was beaten.

# CHAPTER 3

Thursday sped by. Friday came. After school Bertie played in his room with his pet earthworm, Arthur. Bertie kept him in a goldfish bowl filled with mud, leaves and a plastic soldier for company. He was trying to train Arthur to come when he called him. "Arthur! Arthur!" he coaxed.

# Dirty Bertie

"Bertie!" called Mum from downstairs.

"Just a minute!" shouted Bertie. He hid the bowl under the bed. His mum didn't exactly know about Arthur yet. A moment later she poked her head round the door.

"Come on, Bertie! You'll be late for the party."

"What party?"

"That's not going to work," said Mum.

"But … but … I haven't got a present," said Bertie, desperately.

Mum held up two boxes. "The doll or the face paints?" she said.

"Face paints," said Bertie, gloomily. He wasn't going to turn up holding a doll.

"Oh, and I bought you this to wear." Mum handed him a brand new T-shirt.

"Blech!" said Bertie. "It's pink. I can't wear that!"

# Dirty Bertie

"Don't be silly, Bertie, it's a pink party. Now hurry up and get ready." She disappeared, leaving him with the pink horror.

Bertie retrieved Arthur from under the bed. He held the T-shirt against him and looked in the mirror.

"What do you think, Arthur?" he asked. "Yucky or what?"

# Dirty Bertie

Suddenly Bertie had the most brilliant brainwave. The invitation said to wear something pink. Well, worms were pink, weren't they? He could go to the party as an earthworm! All he needed was something pink and wormy to wear.

Bertie tiptoed into his parents' room. Strictly speaking he wasn't allowed in there, not since he'd used Mum's favourite perfume to make a stinkbomb.

Opening the wardrobe, he began to pull out armfuls of clothes. Nothing pink there. But then – bingo! – on top of the wardrobe he spotted something. Suzy's sleeping bag, the one she was taking to school camp. It was bright pink with a hood that fitted snugly over your head – perfect for an earthworm. All it needed was the finishing touch.

# Dirty Bertie

Ten minutes later Bertie's mum found him in the back garden.

"Oh, Bertie! No, Bertie!" she wailed.

"What?" said Bertie.

"You're filthy. Look at you!"

Bertie scrambled to his feet and inspected his costume. He was impressively dirty – but that was the whole point of rolling in a flowerbed.

"Earthworms are meant to be muddy," he explained. "They live underground."

"Bertie! I asked you to get ready for the party!"

"I am. It said to go in pink, so I am. I'm going as an earthworm."

Mum looked closer. "What is that?" she said. "It's not Suzy's sleeping bag?"

"It is!" beamed Bertie. "It's perfect!"

The sleeping bag was smeared with mud. It covered Bertie from head to toe with only his grimy face peeping out. Mum sat down heavily on the rockery.

"Bertie, you can't go like that."

"Why not?" said Bertie. "It's pink. I bet no one else'll be going as an earthworm."

"No," sighed Mum, wearily. "I doubt if they will."

# CHAPTER 4

Angela's front door was festooned with pink balloons. Mum walked up the path with Bertie hopping after her like a giant pink jumping bean and rang the doorbell. Mrs Nicely came to the door.

"Hello!" she said and then, "Oh good heavens!" as her eye fell on Bertie.

"I'm an earthworm," Bertie explained.

# Dirty Bertie

"How … ah … lovely, Bertie," said Mrs Nicely. "Do come in."

Bertie showered clods of earth on to the carpet as he bounced into the hall.

Most of Angela's friends had come as princesses and fairies. The front room was a sea of pink tutus.

"You're here, Bertie!" said Angela, running up to him. "I'm a fairy. Look, I've got wings!"

"I'm an earthworm," said Bertie. "I got you a present."

An arm emerged from the sleeping bag holding a scruffy package. Angela tore off the wrapping paper. "Thank you!" she trilled, dropping the face paints on top of her big pile of presents. Bertie gazed at them longingly.

"Let's play a game," said Mrs Nicely.

# Dirty Bertie

"Who wants to play Musical Statues?"

"Me! Me!" chorused the fairies and princesses.

The music played and they all danced round the room.

"Bertie isn't dancing!" moaned Angela.

"Yes I am," said Bertie. "This is how earthworms dance!"

Bertie rolled over and over on the floor so that the dancing fairies had to jump over him. The music suddenly stopped.

# Dirty Bertie

"Statues everybody! Statues!" cried
Mrs Nicely. The fairies and princesses
became wobbling statues. But Bertie,
who was feeling a little hot and dizzy,
hadn't been listening. He just kept rolling
… straight into one of the fairies.

Laura wobbled and fell into Angela…
Angela wobbled and fell on top of
Maisie and Clare…

Soon all the statues had collapsed in a
heap. Bertie rolled to a halt at Mrs
Nicely's feet. "Did I win?" he asked.

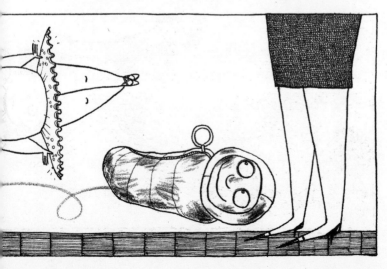

# Dirty Bertie

Tea was pink. Pink biscuits, pink
ice cream and a pink birthday cake in
the shape of a heart. Bertie ate "worm-
style" by licking things off his plate.

"Bertie, please don't slurp like that,"
sighed Mrs Nicely.

"Sorry," replied Bertie. "Worms can't
help it. They don't know about manners."

# Dirty Bertie

When tea was over Mrs Nicely surveyed the mess on the floor. Most of it had collected under Bertie's chair.

"Can we go on the bouncy castle now?" asked Bertie, tugging at her sleeve.

"In a minute, Bertie!" she said. "Angela, why don't you all go next door and play with your presents?"

While Angela's friends played with her Little Patty Pony set, Bertie eyed the face paints. Maybe he would just try one? He wriggled an arm out of his sleeping bag and selected a black face paint. He drew on his chin and looked in the mirror. Next he drew on his cheeks. Perhaps he would turn himself into a vampire or a zombie? Or better still…

He was so busy that he didn't notice the room had gone quiet.

# Dirty Bertie

# Dirty Bertie

"Oh Bertie!" said Angela.

"Ah," said Bertie, "I was just … um … borrowing them."

"What have you done to your face?"

"I'm a slug," said Bertie.

"You said you were a worm."

"I was, but now I'm a slug. A big black, slimy slug."

He slithered on to the floor, making slimy, sluggy noises. Angela's friends shrieked with delight and ran to hide behind the curtains. Angela peeped out, her eyes shining. "Make me a slug too, Bertie," she pleaded.

Mrs Nicely was still tidying up when the doorbell rang. Thank goodness it was over for another year. She went to answer the door. Bertie's mum stood on the doorstep with three other parents.

"I do hope Bertie's behaved himself," she said.

"Oh yes," said Mrs Nicely. "He's such a … lively boy." She led them through to the back door. "They're all playing in the garden," she said. "Angela's had such a lovely time. They've all been good as…"

Mrs Nicely stopped in her tracks. Eight children were bouncing on the bouncy castle. But the princesses and fairies who had come to the party had vanished. In their place were ugly green monsters in filthy tutus who looked like they'd crawled from a swamp.

In the middle of them all was Bertie, bouncing and whooping.

# Dirty Bertie

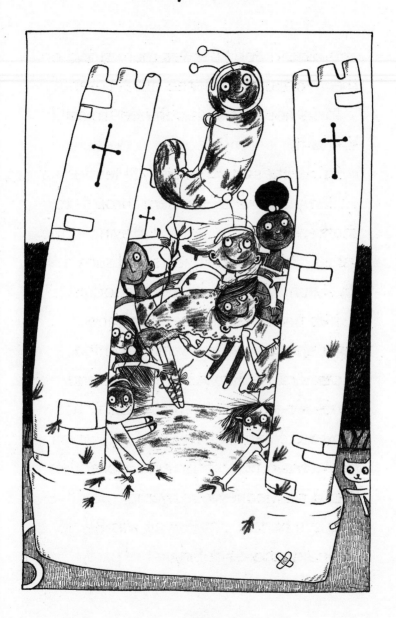

"Look, Mum!" sang Angela. "I'm a creepy caterpillar! Bertie did it!"

Mrs Nicely looked at Bertie's mum. The other parents looked at Bertie's mum. Bertie's mum looked at Bertie.

"What?" said Bertie.

Back in his room, Bertie was glad to be reunited with Arthur. Personally he couldn't see why everyone had made such a fuss. What was the point of giving someone face paints if they weren't allowed to use them?

"Anyway," he told Arthur with a smile. "I don't think they'll be inviting me next year."

He considered it. Really the party hadn't turned out so badly.

# Dirty Bertie

He felt in his pocket and brought out
something pink and sticky.

"Look, Arthur!" he said. "I saved you
some cake!"

# CHAPTER 1

Bertie had no manners. His family all agreed. He lolled, he fidgeted and talked with his mouth full. He sniffed and slurped and burped and picked his nose.

"Bertie, use a hanky!"

"Take your elbows off the table!"

"Don't touch that, it's dirty, Bertie!" his parents moaned every day.

# Dirty Bertie

Bertie didn't see the point. Animals didn't make all this fuss. Did pigs or dogs have manners? When Whiffer weed against a tree no one seemed to mind. Yet if Bertie had done that his mum would have fainted on the spot.

No, in Bertie's opinion manners were a waste of time. But that was before he heard about the prize.

It was the head teacher, Miss Skinner, who had announced the prize in assembly one morning.

"Does anyone know what tomorrow is?" she asked. Her gaze fell on Bertie who was crossing his eyes at Darren.

"Bertie!" she said.

"Uh … yes, Miss?"

**44**

# Dirty Bertie

"Do you know what tomorrow is?"

Bertie thought. "Tuesday?" he said.

Miss Skinner gave him one of her looks. "Tomorrow," she said, "is National Courtesy Day. It's a day when we should be especially polite, so I want us all to think about our manners. We are lucky to have Miss Prim from the library coming to visit us, and she has agreed to present a very special prize to the child with the best manners."

"Huh! Special prize!" said Bertie to Darren as they trooped back to the classroom. "I bet it's some boring old book about being polite."

"Actually it's not," said a reedy voice behind them. It was Know-All Nick, Bertie's worst enemy.

"How do you know?" asked Bertie.

# Dirty Bertie

"Because I heard Miss Skinner tell Miss Boot," said Nick, looking pleased with himself. "She said the tickets had come this morning."

"Tickets for what?" asked Darren.

"Wouldn't you like to know!" sneered Nick (who would have liked to know himself).

"I bet it's football tickets!" said Darren.

"Or cinema tickets," said Donna.

"Or tickets for Mega Mayhem," said Bertie, his eyes lighting up. Mega Mayhem was the best theme park in the world and he'd been begging to go for months.

"It doesn't matter what it is," said Nick, smugly. "I'm bound to win. My mum says I've got beautiful manners."

"It's a pity your face is so ugly," muttered Bertie.

# Dirty Bertie

Bertie thought about the prize for the rest of the day. He was sure the tickets were for Mega Mayhem and he'd made up his mind to win them. Even if it meant he had to be polite for a whole day he didn't care. After all, how hard could it be?

# CHAPTER 2

The next morning Bertie bounded out of bed. Today was National Courtesy Day – the day he was going to win the prize. On the landing he met his mum returning from the bathroom.

"Good morning, Mum," he said. "Isn't it a lovely morning?"

His mum gave him a suspicious look.

"What have you done, Bertie?"

"I haven't done anything," said Bertie. "I was just being polite."

Downstairs Dad and Suzy were eating breakfast.

"Good morning!" Bertie greeted them cheerfully, as he sat down.

He poured Frostie Flakes into his bowl and cleared his throat. "Ahem. Would you pass the milk please, Suzy?"

Suzy stared at him. "Why are you talking in that funny way?"

"It's not a funny way, thank you. It's called being polite."

Bertie poured milk into his bowl without spilling a drop and sucked his Frostie Flakes so as not to make a noise. Even when he dropped his spoon he was careful to wipe it on his jumper before putting it in his mouth.

"I might be getting a prize today," he announced.

Dad looked up. "Mmm? What kind of prize?"

"For being polite," said Bertie. "It's National Courtesy Day and they're giving a prize for being polite."

"You? Polite? HA!" snorted Suzy.

Bertie sniffed. "I'm more polite than you, fat-face."

"Nose, Bertie," said Dad. "Where's your hanky?"

Bertie pulled a grubby hanky from his pocket and wiped his nose. Something fell out and plopped into the sugar bowl.

# Dirty Bertie

"Eugghh!" shrieked Suzy. "What's that?"

"It's only Buzz. He won't hurt you," said Bertie, picking out the large bluebottle.

"Bertie! It's a dead fly!" said Dad.

# Dirty Bertie

"I know," replied Bertie. "Don't worry, I'm going to bury him."

Bertie had found Buzz lying on his window sill. He had decided to bury him under the apple tree. He blew off the sugar that was stuck to his wings.

"Put it away!" said Dad. "It's filthy!"

Bertie sighed and wrapped Buzz inside his hanky. He would bury him after school. That was the trouble he thought, you did your best to be polite and all you got was people shouting at you.

# CHAPTER 3

Miss Prim stood at the front of the class. She was tall and thin. Her glasses hung round her neck on a cord. Bertie thought she must be a hundred at least. He'd seen Miss Prim at the library where she stood behind a desk and stamped people's books. He hoped she didn't remember him. Last time he'd been to the library Whiffer had done something in the story corner and they'd had to leave quickly.

"This is Miss Prim," said Miss Boot. "I hope we're all going to show her how well-mannered we can be." She ran her eye over her class, who were all sitting up straight and paying attention. It was marvellous the effect a prize could have. Even Bertie wasn't lolling in his seat or pushing a pencil up his nose.

Miss Prim talked to the class about the importance of good manners. Bertie tried to listen but his mind kept drifting off. He was imagining whizzing down the Slide of Doom at Mega Mayhem.

"Now," said Miss Boot. "Who would like to show our visitor around the school? Let's have two volunteers."

# Dirty Bertie

Bertie's hand shot in the air. This was his chance to show Miss Prim how polite he could be. Unfortunately everyone else in his class had the same idea. Thirty children strained out of their seats waving their hands in the air. "Miss! Ooh, Miss! Please, Miss!"

# Dirty Bertie

Miss Boot pointed. "Nick. I'm sure you'll look after our visitor."

Bertie couldn't believe it. Not Know-All Nick – why did he always get picked? Just because he'd made Miss Boot a soppy card on her birthday. It wasn't fair – Bertie never got picked for anything.

Miss Boot hesitated. She needed someone else who was polite and reliable.

"Miss, ooh, Miss! Me, Miss!"

"What about that boy at the back who's sitting so quietly?" suggested Miss Prim.

"Oh," said Miss Boot. "Not Bertie?"

Bertie, who hadn't been listening, looked up. "Me?" he said.

# Dirty Bertie

Miss Prim walked down the corridor, admiring the paintings on the walls.

"That one's mine," said Nick, pointing to a bright picture of a sunset.

"And that one's mine," said Bertie, pointing to a splodgy mess of green. "It's an alien. And that's his dinner inside him."

"Ah," said Miss Prim. "How unusual. Don't we have a hanky, Bertie?"

"Oh yes. 'Scuse me," said Bertie. He pulled out his hanky and offered it to Miss Prim.

"No, I meant you. You need to wipe your nose!"

"Oh. Thanks," said Bertie. He wiped his nose on his sleeve and pocketed his hanky. He'd just remembered Buzz was wrapped inside and he didn't want him falling out.

# Dirty Bertie

Miss Prim sighed heavily. "Perhaps we could look in the next class," she said.

Nick started to walk ahead quickly. Bertie kept pace with him. There was a mad dash for the door and they both grabbed the handle at once.

"I was first!"

"I was!"

"I was!"

Miss Prim caught up with them. "Boys, boys! I hope we're not squabbling," she said.

"Oh no," smiled Nick. "I was just telling Bertie his shirt's hanging out."

Bertie looked behind him. Nick wrenched open the door, squashing Bertie behind it.

# Dirty Bertie

"After you, Miss," said Nick. Miss Prim
beamed at him.

"Thank you, Nicholas. It's nice to see
someone remembers their manners."

# CHAPTER 4

By lunchtime Bertie was exhausted. Being polite was hard work, especially with Know-All Nick trying to outdo him the whole time. And now it looked as if he was stuck with Miss Prim for lunch.

As they crossed the hall, Bertie could hardly believe his eyes. No one in the dinner queue was pushing and shoving.

# Dirty Bertie

There was no running or fighting or firing peas across the room. Everyone was eating their lunch quietly and politely.

"Hello, Miss Prim!" called Donna, as they passed by.

Bertie gulped. Three of his teachers were waiting for them at a table laid with a white tablecloth and a vase of flowers.

"Do come and join us," said Miss Skinner. "Bertie will fetch your lunch."

"Careful you don't drop it, Bertie!" whispered Know-All Nick.

"Careful I don't drop it on you," muttered Bertie.

Bertie sat opposite Miss Prim and Know-All Nick and stared at the plate in front of him. Spaghetti – how was he meant to eat that without making a mess? He watched Miss Prim wind spaghetti round her fork and tried to copy her. The spaghetti fell off before it reached his mouth. Nick put a hand over his mouth and loudly sucked up a piece of spaghetti. "Shloooooop!"

"Bertie!" he said. "Don't be so disgusting!"

# Dirty Bertie

The teachers all looked in Bertie's direction.

"But … it wasn't me!" gasped Bertie. "It was him!"

Miss Prim made a tutting noise. "Don't tell tales, Bertie, it isn't nice."

Bertie turned to glare at Nick. He would have liked to put spaghetti down his neck. He would have liked to pour a jug of water down his pants. But he wanted those tickets and Miss Prim was watching him like a hawk. As he lifted his fork to his mouth a hand jogged his elbow.

SPLAT! A splodge of sauce landed on the white tablecloth.

"Oh Bertie, you are messy!" jeered Nick. "Look what you've done!"

Miss Prim made another tutting noise.

# Dirty Bertie

"But it wasn't ME!" shouted Bertie.

Miss Boot glared.

Bertie ground his teeth. He would get that two-faced slimy sneak.

Nick was sent to fetch dessert.

Bertie's eyes lit up. Chocolate fudge cake – his favourite. He reached out to grab a piece.

"Manners, Bertie," Miss Prim reminded him. "We don't grab, we offer the plate to others."

Bertie reluctantly passed the cake round the table. Miss Skinner took a slice, so did Miss Boot and Mr Plumly. Bertie watched anxiously as the cake began to disappear.

"Oh dear," said Miss Prim, helping herself. "Only one piece left! Which of you is going to have it?"

# Dirty Bertie

Bertie looked at Nick. Nick looked at Bertie. Both of them eyed the last slice of fudge cake. Then Nick did a surprising thing – he offered the plate to Bertie.

"You have it, Bertie," he said with a sickly smile. "I don't mind, really."

Bertie wasn't going to fall for that one. "That's okay, Nick, I want you to have it."

"Oh, well, if you insist," said Nick. "We don't want it going to waste." He snatched the last piece and took a large bite. "Thanks, Bertie."

# Dirty Bertie

Bertie glared furiously. He'd been tricked! Well, that was it. No more manners, this was war. That fudge cake was his by right and he was going to get it back. Bertie reached into his pocket and brought out his hanky. Nick was too busy talking to Miss Prim to notice a hand dart across the table.

"Any second now," thought Bertie. "Five, four, three, two…"

Nick reached for the cake and raised it to his mouth. There was something black on top.

"ARGHHHHH! A fly!" screamed Nick, dropping the cake on the table.

"ARGGHHHH!" shrieked Miss Prim as Buzz landed in front of her.

"I'll get it!" cried Miss Skinner. She seized a spoon and attacked the bluebottle.

# Dirty Bertie

SMACK! WHACK! THUMP! Plates and cups leaped in the air. Buzz hopped and jumped with each blow, showing surprising speed for a dead fly.

Miss Boot grabbed the water jug and emptied it over the table. SPLOOSH!

Buzz lay still in a puddle with his legs in the air.

"Is it dead?" asked Miss Skinner. She picked up the fly by one leg and examined it.

# Dirty Bertie

The silence was broken by a loud burp.

Six pairs of eyes turned on Bertie. He had cake crumbs round his mouth and a satisfied smile on his face.

"Bertie!" said Miss Skinner.

"Um… Pardon me!" said Bertie, politely. He held out his hand. "Could I have my fly back, please?"

# Dirty Bertie

Later that afternoon Bertie crowded into the hall with everyone else. The moment had arrived for Miss Prim to announce the winner of the prize. Bertie knew he didn't stand a chance – not after all the trouble at lunchtime. At least he'd been able to rescue Buzz from the litter bin. In any case it had all been worth it to see the look on Know-All Nick's face when he'd come eye to eye with Buzz. Bertie didn't mind who won the prize – as long as it wasn't Nick.

"And the winner," said Miss Prim, "is Nicholas Payne."

Bertie groaned. Know-All Nick made his way to the front and shook Miss Prim's hand. Everyone craned their necks to see what his prize would be. Miss Prim handed him an envelope. "As you're always so polite I'm sure you're going to love this. It's two tickets for the Museum of Manners in London."

Nick turned white. His mouth gaped open but nothing came out.

Bertie leaned forward. "Manners, Nick," he said. "Aren't you going to say thank you?"

# CHAPTER 1

RUMBLE, RUMBLE! SCREECH! SNORT!

Something was making a noise outside Bertie's window. He sat up in bed. It was Saturday, Bertie's favourite day of the week. Saturday was bin day. He pulled back his curtains. Sure enough, there was the dustcart at the far end of the road. If he hurried he would be just in time.

# Dirty Bertie

Downstairs he found Mum making tea in the kitchen.

"Morning, Bertie…" She broke off and stared at him. "What on earth are you wearing?"

Bertie looked at his outfit. He had on his dad's painting overalls, a woolly hat and a muddy pair of wellingtons. True, the overalls were a bit big, but Bertie thought they were perfect for a bin man.

# Dirty Bertie

"It's Saturday," he said. "I've got to help Ed with the bins."

"Oh Bertie, not today," sighed Mum.

"Why not?"

"It's the summer fair this morning. I don't want you getting filthy."

"That's why I'm wearing these!" said Bertie, flapping his long sleeves.

"Anyway," said Mum, "you're too late. I took the rubbish out last night."

"But I always do it!" cried Bertie.

"Sorry, I forgot. You can do it next time."

He stared after his mum as she disappeared upstairs with her tea. Whiffer looked up from a bone he was licking and blinked at him. "How could she forget?" asked Bertie. "I always take the rubbish out on Saturdays!"

# Dirty Bertie

When he grew up Bertie had decided
he wanted to be a bin man. He wanted
to wear an orange jacket and big gloves
and ride in a truck that snorted like a
dragon. Most of all he wanted to work
with mountains of messy, smelly, sticky
rubbish. Bertie loved rubbish. He had
piles of it under his bed. String, lolly
sticks, rubber bands, sweet wrappers –
it was amazing what people threw away!

He began to rummage in the drawers.
The bin men would be here any minute.
Finally he found what he was looking for
– a large black bin bag. All he needed
now was a few bits of rubbish to fill it.
Bertie looked around.

In went a dishcloth, a bar of soap, a tin
of cat food and a pile of letters from
Bertie's school (no one ever read them

anyway). In went his dad's slippers, some carrots (yuck!), a cauliflower (double yuck!) and his sister's pony magazine.

Rumble, rumble! The dustcart was coming. Bertie scooted into the hall dragging his bag behind him. Someone had left a pot of old flowers by the front door ready to throw out. Bertie scooped it into the bag with the rest.

# Dirty Bertie

The wheelie bin stood on the pavement. Bertie climbed on to the front wall so he could reach to drop his bag in. He peered into the bin, sniffing the sweet smell of rotting vegetables.

In one corner he caught sight of something familiar. Wasn't that his chewing gum collection? Surely his mum hadn't thrown it out? He bent into the bin to try and rescue it. The jar was just out of reach of his fingertips. He'd have to… "ARGHHH!" Bertie toppled in head first.

# Dirty Bertie

His face was wedged against something soft and squashy. "Mmff! Help!"

"Hello, mate," said a voice. "Having a bit of trouble there?" Strong hands pulled him out and set him on his feet.

"Oh dear!" grinned Ed. "Your mum's going to be pleased."

Bertie inspected himself. He did seem to have got a bit messy. There was something sticky on his overalls that smelled like tomato ketchup. He brushed off some tea leaves and straightened his hat. A piece of potato peel fell off. He held up the rescued jam-jar to show Ed.

"I was looking for this. It's my chewing gum collection," he explained. "I'm doing an experiment to see what happens when it gets really old."

"And what does happen?" Ed asked.

# Dirty Bertie

"It goes hard and it tastes really disgusting," said Bertie. "Want to try a bit?"

"No thanks," smiled Ed. "I've got to get on. Want to give me a hand?"

"Yes please!" said Bertie. "I brought you an extra bag today."

Bertie presented him with the rubbish he'd collected. Ed dropped the bag in the wheelie bin and Bertie pulled it to the waiting truck. He watched fascinated as the truck opened its metal jaws and swallowed up the rubbish. Ed held out a gloved hand and Bertie shook it.

"Good work, mate," said Ed. "See you next week." He moved off down the road, whistling.

"See you!" called Bertie.

# CHAPTER 2

Back in the house, Bertie whistled as he spooned dog food into Whiffer's bowl. He whistled as he took off his overalls and sat down to have some breakfast.

"Bertie, please!" said Dad.

"What?" said Bertie. "I'm only whistling."

"That isn't whistling. You sound like you've got a puncture."

# Dirty Bertie

"Well I've got to practise," said Bertie. "How can I learn to whistle if you don't let me practise?"

Mum came into the kitchen looking flustered.

"Bertie, have you seen my flower arrangement? I left it by the front door this morning."

Bertie paused with his finger in the peanut butter. "By the door?"

# Dirty Bertie

"Yes, it's for the competition at the summer fair. I spent hours working on it and now it's disappeared. Are you sure you haven't seen it?"

"Me? Um … no."

"Are you all right? You look a bit pale."

"I'm fine," said Bertie, who suddenly wasn't feeling so well. He remembered the pot of old flowers by the front door. He remembered putting it in his rubbish bag. Uh oh – the dustcart must have eaten it. Now he thought about it his mum had been going on about the competition for weeks. First prize always went to Mrs Nicely next door, but this year Bertie's mum felt she stood a chance. Or she would have done… How was Bertie to know the flowers by the door were hers? They looked practically dead!

He got up from the table and sidled towards the door.

"Where are you going?" asked Mum. "You haven't finished your breakfast."

"I just need to do something."

"And what's this all over Dad's overalls?"

"Just ketchup. I had a bit of an accident."

"Bertie…!"

But Bertie was making for the door. If he was going to get those flowers back he would need to move fast.

# CHAPTER 3

Bertie bent over the handlebars of his bike, pedalling at top speed. Whiffer scampered behind, trying to keep up. Maybe he was too late already. Even if he caught up with the dustcart, how was he going to get the flowers back? Ed had told him all the dustcarts took their loads to an enormous dump.

# Dirty Bertie

Perhaps Ed would let him hunt through the mountains of rubbish there? Bertie loved the idea of that. But at the end of the road there was no sign of either Ed or the truck. By now it might be miles away. He sped on towards the park and slammed on his brakes at the corner. There, parked a hundred metres away, was the dustcart.

"Hey!" called Bertie. "Hey, wait a minute!"

The truck was starting to pull away. It got up speed, turned a corner and vanished out of sight. Bertie looked down at Whiffer whose ears drooped in sympathy.

He was sunk. Mum would scream. Dad would shout. He would be sent to his room for a million years.

# Dirty Bertie

"Bertie, is that you?" called Mum as he
crept in through the front door.

"No," answered Bertie.

"I want a word with you. Now."

Bertie drooped into the kitchen
where Mum, Dad and Suzy were waiting
for him. He could tell by their faces that
he'd been rumbled.

# Dirty Bertie

"Where are my slippers?" said Dad.

"Where's my *Pony Weekly*?" asked
Suzy.

"And what have you done with my
flower arrangement?" demanded Mum.

"Me? Why do I always get the blame?"
protested Bertie. "It's not my fault if
people keep losing things!"

Mum folded her arms. "Look at me,
Bertie. I want the truth. Did you touch
those flowers?"

Bertie tried to look at his mum.
"I might have um … given them to
someone," he mumbled.

"I told you!" said Suzy.

"Who?" demanded Mum.

Bertie tried to think of an answer. He
wanted to tell the truth but the truth
was he'd given the flowers to a dustcart.

By now they were probably buried under six feet of cabbages and nappies.

"I gave them to … Gran!" he said with sudden inspiration.

"Gran? What on earth for?"

"She likes flowers," said Bertie. "She likes smelling them and stuff."

Mum looked unconvinced. "And when did you do this?"

"This morning," said Bertie. "I saw them by the front door and I thought I'd take them to Gran to cheer her up."

His family stared at him. Bertie had never given flowers to anyone before. On the other hand, he had been known to do all sorts of weird things. Mum's expression softened a bit.

"Well it was a nice thought, Bertie, but I need those flowers back. They've got to be at the church hall by ten. I'll give Gran a ring."

She picked up the phone.

"No!" said Bertie, desperately. "I'll go round! It'll be quicker. She's probably finished smelling them by now."

Mum replaced the phone. "All right, but you'd better hurry. If I miss this competition you're in serious trouble."

# Dirty Bertie

Bertie set off with Whiffer padding beside him. At the end of the road he sat down on a wall to think. Now what was he going to do? Bringing Gran into it had only made things worse. Now Mum expected him to come back with her stupid flower arrangement. He stared gloomily at Whiffer who was sniffing around the garden behind him. The house was empty and the front garden overgrown with tall weeds.

Suddenly Bertie had a brilliant idea. What was to stop him making his own

flower arrangement? It would be easy!
There were hundreds of flowers right
here that nobody wanted. All he had to
do was pick a handful, stick them in a
pot and enter it in the competition. If he
took it to the church hall himself, his
mum might never find out.

Half an hour later Bertie had put his
plan into operation. The new flower
arrangement had been safely delivered
to the hall. He hurried home to tell his
mum the good news.

## CHAPTER 4

The summer fair was in full swing when
Bertie and his family arrived. He trailed
round the stalls with Whiffer on his lead.
There were stalls selling plants and
home-made jam but nothing to interest
Bertie. For some reason, Whiffer kept
whining and pulling him back to the table
displaying the flower arrangements.

# Dirty Bertie

Mrs Nicely was standing by the table, talking to Bertie's mum. "I don't know what I'd do if I won again," she was saying. "It would be too embarrassing."

"I can imagine," said Bertie's mum. "So which one is yours?"

"Oh, that little vase of tiger lilies," said Mrs Nicely, pointing to a towering display of yellow blooms. She lowered her voice and pointed. "Can you believe someone actually entered that ghastly mess?"

# Dirty Bertie

Bertie stared at the "ghastly mess".
It was a cracked pot with dandelions,
grass and twigs sticking out in all
directions. In the middle was what
looked like a dog's bone.

"Actually," said Bertie, loudly, "I think
that's the best of them all."

Mum pulled him to one side. "Bertie,
where's my flower arrangement?
I thought you said you gave it in."

"Um … I did," said Bertie. Luckily, at that moment, he was interrupted by one of the judges.

"Can I have your attention? We're about to announce the results of the flower arranging competition," he boomed.

Second prize went to Mrs Nicely who tried hard not to look disappointed. First prize went to Mr Pye's bowl of roses.

"Finally," said the judge, "the prize for the most original display. This year we felt one entry beautifully captured our theme of 'Wild Nature'."

The judge held up a pot. It was Bertie's pot. "The winner," he said, "is Mrs Burns."

"That's us!" shouted Bertie, excitedly. Whiffer barked and strained on his lead, trying to reach his bone.

Mum looked at Bertie and then in

horror at the scruffy pot of weeds the judge was holding. "Bertie, that is *not* my flower arrangement," she hissed.

"No," admitted Bertie. "I had to make a few um … changes."

"Go on," Dad whispered to Mum. "They're all waiting."

Mum stepped forward to collect her prize, her face a deep shade of pink.

"Tell me," said the judge. "I'm curious. What gave you the idea of using a bone? Most original."

Mum shot a dark look at Bertie. "Oh it was my son's idea really. He can make a dog's dinner of anything."

"I've never been so embarrassed in all my life," moaned Mum on the way home. "Mrs Nicely looked as if she was going to explode."

Bertie couldn't see what she was complaining about. After all, she wanted to win a prize and she had. You would have thought she'd be grateful! In any case things had worked out pretty well. His mum had won a gardening kit, which included a large pair of green gardening gloves. Bertie was wearing them now. They were the perfect thing for a bin man.

# Dirty Bertie

## FLEAS!

For Jane, for all your scootering across
London on your moped to collect
and deliver *Bertie* bits and pieces.
A big thank you ~ D R

For Laurie, who's not as dirty as he'd
like to be ~ A M

# Contents

# CHAPTER 1

SCRATCH! SCRATCH! SCRATCH!

Bertie was reading his comic at the table.

"Bertie do you have to do that?" asked Mum.

"What?"

"Keep scratching like that. You're worse than a dog."

"I can't help it, I'm itchy," said Bertie.

He went back to his comic.

Scratch! Scratch! He scratched his leg under the table. Scratch! Scratch! He scratched under his pyjama top. Scratch! Scratch! He itched his arm.

"BERTIE! What's wrong with you?" said Mum.

"Sorry," shrugged Bertie. "I'm itchy all over."

"Let me take a look at you," said Mum. She rolled up his sleeve to inspect his arm. A look of horror appeared on her face. "Oh no! Fleas!"

"FLEAS?" cried Suzy.

"FLEAS?" cried Dad.

"Where? I can't see them!" said Bertie, peering at his arm curiously. Mum pointed at the tiny red dots above his elbow.

"There," she said. "Those are flea bites."

Suzy shifted her chair away from
Bertie. "Ugh! Keep away! I don't want
your fleas."

She scratched her hair. Maybe her
grubby little brother had given her fleas
already. Maybe she had flea bites all over
her! She fled from the table and dashed
upstairs to the bathroom.

"But where did he get them?" asked
Dad.

"I bet I can guess," said Mum, grimly.

# Dirty Bertie

Whiffer was in the lounge, dozing peacefully in an armchair. Scratch! Scratch! Scratch! His back leg swished like a windscreen wiper.

"There!" said Mum. "Just as I thought. There's the fleabag."

Bertie bent over to take a closer look. It was true. Whiffer's fur was alive with tiny black creatures hopping around like … well, like fleas.

"Good grief!" said Mum. "He's crawling with them!"

"Wow! Millions!" said Bertie.

"Enough to start a flea circus," muttered Dad, keeping his distance.

"What's a flea circus?" asked Bertie.

"Oh you used to get them years ago," said Dad. "Performing fleas – doing tricks and things."

Bertie could hardly believe his ears. A flea circus! With performing fleas! What a fantastic idea! He'd already tried to train his pet earthworm, but Mum had put a stop to that when she found Arthur in his bed. But fleas? That was a much better idea. Fleas could jump and hop so surely they could be trained to do other things? Like acrobatics. Fleas turning somersaults.

Fleas standing on each other's
shoulders. Fleas flying through the air on
a flea trapeze! All he had to do was
catch some of Whiffer's fleas and he
could have his very own circus.

# Dirty Bertie

Mum had Whiffer by the collar and was pulling him out of the armchair.

"We've got to do something," she said. "Fleas spread. They lay their eggs everywhere. They're probably all over the furniture by now!"

Just thinking about it made Dad feel itchy. "How do you get rid of them?" he asked.

Mum dragged Whiffer through the kitchen and out of the back door.

"You can buy flea shampoo – but someone will have to bath him."

"I'll do it!" said Bertie.

"NO!" said both his parents at once.

"He'll have to go to the vets," said Mum, eyeing Dad. "You can take him."

"Why me?" said Dad. "I took him last time!"

# Dirty Bertie

Dad remembered their last visit all too well. The vet had tried to force a pill down Whiffer's throat. Whiffer had spat it out three times.

"Well I can't do it," said Mum flatly. "I'm taking Suzy shopping this morning."

"But I've got work to do!" protested Dad.

"This is an emergency," said Mum. "The house is crawling with fleas. Bertie's already been bitten. They won't just walk out of the door, you know."

"All right, all right," groaned Dad. "I'll take him."

# CHAPTER 2

Bertie waited till Mum and Suzy had gone out. He crept out of the back door, armed with his flea collecting kit. Whiffer wagged his tail, pleased to see him.

Bertie crouched beside him with a toothbrush and a matchbox. With a little coaxing he managed to get a few of the fleas on the end of the toothbrush.

He shook them into the matchbox and slid the lid shut quickly.

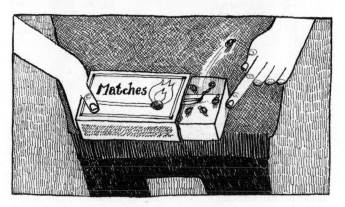

"BERTIE!" called Dad from indoors. "Can you come here a minute?"

Bertie stuffed the matchbox into his pocket and went inside.

Dad was working at the computer in the back room.

"Bertie," he said. "Are you busy right now?"

"Not especially," said Bertie.

"I was thinking. Maybe you'd like to

take Whiffer to the vets? He's your dog."

"No thanks. Can I go now?"

"Wait!" said Dad, desperately. "I'll pay you."

Bertie paused in the doorway. "How much?"

"Two pounds."

Bertie thought about it. As usual he'd spent all his pocket money.

"Three," said Dad. "Okay, five pounds – that's my last offer."

"Done!" said Bertie. He held out his hand.

"Oh no," said Dad. "You don't get paid until the job's done. And you'd better ask Gran to go with you."

Bertie nodded. Five pounds – he could do a lot with that. He was already planning what he needed for his flea circus.

# Dirty Bertie

DING DONG! Bertie rang Gran's doorbell.

"Hello, Bertie!" said Gran, opening the door. "What a nice surprise. Come in!"

"I better not," said Bertie. "Dad wants me to take Whiffer to the V-E-T-S."

"The what?" said Gran.

Bertie lowered his voice. "The vets."

"Oh, the VETS! Why are you whispering?"

"Because I don't want Whiffer to hear. He hates the vets."

Gran looked behind him. "Who's going with you?" she asked.

"Ah," said Bertie. "Well…"

"I see," said Gran. "I'd better get my coat then."

"So what's the matter with Whiffer?"
asked Gran, as they headed up the road
with Whiffer on his lead.

"Oh, nothing much. He's just got fleas."

"FLEAS?" Gran stopped dead.

"Yes," said Bertie. "Loads of them!
You should take a look, Gran – it's like a
flea party!"

# Dirty Bertie

"No thanks," said Gran. "I'll take your word for it." She shook her head. "No wonder your dad didn't want to come. Typical! 'Ask your gran. She'll go to the vets with you!'"

"Shhh!" said Bertie. "Not so loud!"

"Don't be daft, Bertie," said Gran. "He's a dog! He can't understand a word we're saying!"

The dog lead suddenly yanked her backwards and they both turned around. Whiffer had stopped and was lying down on the pavement.

# Dirty Bertie

"See?" said Bertie. "You said the word. Now we'll never get him there."

He clapped his hands. "Come on, Whiffer! Let's go!"

But Whiffer wouldn't budge. Bertie pleaded with him. He spoke in his dog-training voice. He tried to drag Whiffer along by his lead but Whiffer dug in his heels and refused to budge.

"Now what?" sighed Gran.

Bertie tried to think. If they didn't get Whiffer to the vets there'd be no five pound reward.

"Maggots!" he said suddenly.

"Maggots?" said Gran. "The poor dog's got fleas already! Bertie, this isn't one of your harebrained ideas, is it?"

"No," said Bertie. "Trust me, Gran, this will work. When Dad goes fishing he uses maggots. The fish come after them. So what we need is something that Whiffer will come after!"

Gran looked at him. "Why do I get the feeling I'm going to regret this?"

"You won't," said Bertie. "I promise. Just lend me your key."

## CHAPTER 3

Ten minutes later Bertie was back. Gran
stared. He was wearing his helmet and
roller blades, and pulling a bag that
trundled along on two wheels.

"That's my shopping bag!" said Gran.

"I know," said Bertie, beaming. "It's
perfect! And look what I found in
the fridge!"

# Dirty Bertie

He unzipped the bag to reveal a string of sausages. "And that's my supper!" said Gran. "What are you up to?"

"It's simple," explained Bertie. "I skate along with the sausages in the bag. As soon as Whiffer sees them he'll start chasing me. He loves sausages!"

"And what am I doing while you're zooming off with my supper?" asked Gran.

"You hold on to Whiffer's lead," said Bertie. "Don't let him catch the sausages or it won't work."

Gran shook her head. "I must be barmy to listen to you."

Bertie's plan worked perfectly – at least to begin with. Bertie whizzed off on his roller blades with the sausages trailing from the shopping bag. As soon as Whiffer spotted them he barked and sprang to his feet. Then he was off, dragging Gran behind him at turbo speed.

"Hang on, Gran!" Bertie called over his shoulder.

"I am hanging on!" puffed Gran. "Can't you tell him to slow down?"

Bertie skated through the precinct, weaving in and out of shoppers. Whiffer bounded along behind, tugging at his lead and barking excitedly. People stopped to stare at the old lady chasing a dog who was chasing a string of sausages.

Everything might have been all right if Whiffer hadn't barked so loudly. But Whiffer always barked when he was excited and he was excited now. As they came tearing down Riddle Road, the Alsatian at Number 12 heard Whiffer barking. Seeing some escaping sausages, he eagerly joined the chase. Further down the road they met the terrier at 47 and the scruffy mongrel at 72. Both of them were fond of sausages and even fonder of a good chase.

# Dirty Bertie

"Help!" cried Gran. "Bertie stop! I'm being attacked!"

Bertie looked behind him. Gran had a pack of dogs snapping at her heels. She was red in the face and skidding along like a tomato on water-skis. Whiffer was gaining on the sausages. Bertie skated faster. He could see the vets at the end of the road.

"Hang on Gran, we're almost there!" he yelled.

Turning sharp left, he whizzed into the drive, up a ramp and through the open door. The receptionist met him in the hall with a pile of files in her arms. Her mouth dropped open.

"I CAN'T STOP!" warned Bertie. He ploughed straight into her, scattering papers everywhere. The shopping bag did a somersault over Bertie's head and the sausages came flying out. A warm, wet tongue licked his face as Whiffer bounded on top of him.

Gran arrived soon after, panting heavily. "Well that worked a treat," she said.

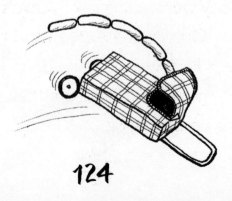

# CHAPTER 4

"Have they gone?" asked Bertie.

Gran glanced out of the window. "No, I'm afraid not."

They were sitting in Mr Cage's waiting room. Outside the Alsatian and his friends kept watch by the door. They had been thrown out once but they weren't giving up that easily.

# Dirty Bertie

The receptionist seemed to think it was all Bertie's fault. She said he had no business bringing every dog in the neighbourhood. Bertie tried to explain they weren't his dogs but the receptionist went on telling him off. Then Gran got cross too, and said if she didn't get a glass of water soon they'd have to call an ambulance.

*At least I got Whiffer to the vets,* thought Bertie. Whiffer was sitting at his feet, happily slobbering over the sausages. It seemed to have escaped his notice that he was in a vet's waiting room. Bertie glanced round the room at the other pets. There was a parrot, a hamster, a snake curled up in a box, and a poodle that looked like a powder puff on legs.

# Dirty Bertie

Scratch! Scratch! Scratch! Whiffer's
back leg was itching again.

The owner of the poodle looked
down her nose at Bertie.
"What's wrong with
your dog?"

"Oh he's fine
really," said Bertie.
"Just a few fleas."

"Fleas? I hope
you're joking?"

"No," said Bertie,
"I can show you if you
like." He reached into his pocket.
But the woman got up from her chair
and quickly backed away. She called to
her poodle.

"Fifi! Fifi, darling! Get away from that
filthy fleabag."

"He's not a filthy fleabag!" said Bertie. "He had a bath last month."

The woman picked up her poodle and sat down on the other side of the room. Bertie and Gran were left sitting by themselves. Gran was chuckling to herself. Bertie hoped that Whiffer had managed to pass a few of his fleas to Fifi.

Just then the door to the street opened and a woman entered, carrying a fat ginger cat. Whiffer looked up and growled. Bertie noticed the door had been left open.

"'Scuse me!" he said. "You'd better shut that! There's some…"

But the warning came too late. The Alsatian and his friends had seen their chance. In a few seconds the waiting room was full of barking, yapping,

growling dogs. The Alsatian chased the
ginger cat round a table. Whiffer and the
terrier snarled and fought over the string
of sausages. And the parrot flew over
their heads squawking, "Give us a kiss!
Give us a kiss!"

"What's the plan now?" shouted Gran in Bertie's ear.

"I'm working on it!" replied Bertie. He tried to catch Whiffer as he ran past.

Hearing the bedlam, Mr Cage came running in and soon wished he hadn't. The cat sprang off the table and sunk its claws into his leg. Whiffer, seeing his old enemy, jumped up and knocked him to the floor. The cat and the barking dogs then used the vet as a roundabout as they chased each other in circles. Finally they escaped out the door with Whiffer leading the way.

There was a long silence as Mr Cage sat up and stared at the wreckage of his waiting room. Bertie bent over him.

"Um, I was wondering," he asked. "Do you know anything about fleas?"

# Dirty Bertie

Dad was still working at the computer when Bertie got home.

"How did it go?" he asked, not looking up.

"Oh," replied Bertie. "It was okay, but—"

"You did get Whiffer to the vets?" Dad interrupted.

"Oh yes, I got him there."

"And you told Mr Cage about the fleas?"

"Yes I told him, but the thing was—"

Dad held up a hand to cut him off. "Tell me later, Bertie, I've just got to finish this." He pulled out a five-pound note from his wallet. "Thanks. And don't mention it to Mum, eh? It can be our secret."

# Dirty Bertie

Bertie took the five-pound note and left. He'd tried to explain but that was the trouble with grown-ups, they never had time to listen. Anyway he had a feeling Mum and Dad would find out the truth soon enough. Perhaps when Mr Cage phoned about the damage. Or when they noticed that Whiffer was still crawling with fleas. So it was probably best to spend the money while he had the chance.

Bertie took the matchbox from his pocket and slid it open a fraction.

"Now," he said, peering inside. "Where could we buy a trapeze?"

# DARE!

# CHAPTER 1

Bertie's class had a new teacher. Mr Weakly was young, pale and very nervous, with round glasses that made him look like a startled owl. He was standing in for Miss Boot while she was off sick. Bertie thought she probably had a sore throat from all that shouting she did.

# Dirty Bertie

He sat at the back of the class whispering with Darren. They were playing the Dare Game. They wouldn't have risked anything so dangerous if Miss Boot had been around. Miss Boot could see you even when her back was turned. But Mr Weakly didn't shout or go purple in the face like Miss Boot; he hardly seemed to get cross at all. Darren had already dared Bertie to burp loudly and Bertie had dared Darren to "drop dead" on the floor. Mr Weakly had merely looked up from his book and asked them not to be silly.

# Dirty Bertie

"So?" said Bertie. "What's the dare?"

"I'm thinking," said Darren. Darren never won the Dare Game because Bertie was daring enough to do anything. Darren had once dared him to shout "Pants!" in assembly and Bertie had yelled it at the top of his voice. But this time he was going to think of something much harder, something that even Bertie wouldn't dare to do. A smile slowly spread across his face. He had it.

"Okay," he said. "I dare you to lock Mr Weakly in the store room."

Bertie gaped at him. "What?"

"That's the dare," said Darren. "I did mine, now it's your turn. Unless you're chickening out."

"Who says I'm chickening out?" said Bertie.

# Dirty Bertie

Bertie glanced over at the store room. It was little more than a tiny cupboard which Miss Boot kept locked at all times. Bertie had been in there once to get some computer paper. It was stuffy and the light didn't work. He wondered if Mr Weakly was scared of the dark… Still, a dare was a dare and he wasn't about to back down.

"All right," he said. "I'll do it."

Bertie's chance came a few minutes later. Mr Weakly took off his reading glasses and asked them to copy some questions into their workbooks. Bertie raised his hand.

"Yes? What is it?" asked Mr Weakly.

"I've run out of space in my workbook, sir," said Bertie.

# Dirty Bertie

"Oh," said Mr Weakly. "Um, what do you normally do?"

"Miss Boot keeps new workbooks in the store room," said Bertie, pointing at the door. "The key's in the drawer."

"Thank you, um…" said Mr Weakly, forgetting Bertie's name. "The rest of you carry on with your work."

Mr Weakly found the key and unlocked the store room door. He disappeared inside, leaving the door open and the key in the lock. Bertie could hear him rummaging on the shelves, looking for the workbooks.

"Go on!" whispered Darren. "Before he comes out!"

Bertie slid out of his seat and crept towards the door. One or two of the class looked up from their work.

# Dirty Bertie

Bertie reached out a hand.

"SLAM!"
The door
swung shut.
"CLICK!"
The key turned
in the lock.
"OH!"
cried Mr
Weakly from
inside.
"What's
happening?"

Bertie pocketed the key and turned
to Darren in triumph. The class were all
staring at him open-mouthed.

"You've locked him in!" said Darren.

"I know," grinned Bertie. "That was
the dare."

"Yeah, but I didn't think you'd actually do it. What are you going to do now?" asked Darren.

Bertie's grin faded – he hadn't really thought that far ahead. He supposed Mr Weakly might be a bit cross. More than a bit in fact. If he'd locked Miss Boot in the store room she would have snorted like a mad bull.

"You're for it," said Donna.

"He's going to kill you," said Know-All Nick.

"No he isn't," said Bertie. "How does he know it was me?"

## CHAPTER 2

THUMP! THUMP! Mr Weakly was knocking on the door.

"Children!" he pleaded. "Really, this isn't funny. I'm going to count to three." He counted to three. "One ... two ... three." Nothing happened.

Eugene looked anxious. "We can't just leave him there," he said.

# Dirty Bertie

"You let him out then," said Darren. "I'm not getting into trouble."

"Why me?" said Eugene. "I didn't lock him in, Bertie did."

They all turned to look at Bertie who had crossed to Mr Weakly's desk.

He had always wondered what it would be like to sit in the teacher's chair. He picked up Mr Weakly's reading glasses and put them on. He added Mr Weakly's jacket.

# Dirty Bertie

"Too much chatter!" he said, sternly. "Get on with your work!"

"You look like a teacher," giggled Donna.

"I am a teacher," said Bertie. "I'm a very strict teacher and you'll all be staying in at playtime if you don't behave!"

The class laughed. Bertie sounded like Miss Boot in a bad mood.

# Dirty Bertie

He peered at them over his glasses. "Who made that pong?" he demanded. "Nick, was that you?"

The class howled with laughter. Know-All Nick turned scarlet.

"You wait. You're in so much trouble," he said. "When Miss Skinner finds out, she'll go up the wall."

# Dirty Bertie

Bertie hadn't thought of Miss Skinner. The head teacher had a nasty habit of looking in on a class unexpectedly. If Miss Skinner found out he'd locked Mr Weakly in the store room there'd be trouble. The thumps were getting louder. Bertie eyed the door. Maybe he should unlock it? If he moved fast he could be back in his seat before Mr Weakly got free. He felt in his pocket. He plunged his hand in deeper. A look of horror crossed his face.

"It's gone!" he said. "I've lost the key!"

"Ha ha!" said Darren. "Come on Bertie, stop messing around."

"I'm not messing around! I put it in my pocket just now."

Bertie turned out his pocket and saw the small hole in the lining.

# Dirty Bertie

The key must have
slipped through and
fallen out. What if he
couldn't find it? What if
Mr Weakly was locked
in the store room *for
ever?*

"Don't just stand there!"
he cried. "Help me look!"

Bertie, Darren and Donna got down
on their hands and knees to search the
floor.

Know-All Nick leaned back in his chair,
smiling. "I told you," he jeered. "You are in
*so* much trouble, Bertie."

Eugene had been keeping watch at
the window. "Hurry up!" he warned.
"Someone's coming!"

"What?" said Bertie.

# Dirty Bertie

The class crowded at the window to look. A woman with wild red hair was striding purposefully across the courtyard towards them.

"Oh her," said Know-all Nick. "She's the school inspector. Miss Skinner said she was coming today."

"Inspector?" said Bertie, horrified. "What's she inspecting?"

"Our school. Weren't you listening in assembly? I expect she wants to inspect Mr Weakly."

They all looked at the store room door. Mr Weakly was rattling the handle.

"We've got to get him out!" said Bertie, starting to panic.

"We?" said Know-All Nick. "You locked him in there, *you* get him out."

"But I can't find the key!" moaned Bertie.

"Do something!" cried Eugene. "She's coming up the stairs."

"Wait, I've got an idea," said Donna. "Bertie can pretend he's our teacher."

"What?" said Bertie.

"Pretend to be Mr Weakly. You're wearing his jacket and glasses. Just say you're him."

"Are you crazy?" said Bertie. "She'll know I'm not him!"

"No she won't, she's probably never

met him. All you have to do is sit at a desk and act like a teacher. You can do it!"

"Yeah," said Darren. "I dare you!"

Bertie shot Darren a look. But maybe Donna was right. He was always doing impressions of Miss Boot, so why couldn't he be Mr Weakly? In any case he didn't have a better idea. He sat down at the teacher's desk. The class were all out of their seats, milling around like lost sheep.

"Well SIT DOWN!" cried Bertie. "Look as if you're working!"

Everyone ran to their desks and sat down. Even Know-All Nick did as he was told. Bertie was amazed at his own power. He gave an order and everyone obeyed him. So this was what it was like to be a teacher!

# CHAPTER 3

Miss Barker knocked on the classroom door and entered. She had heard scuffling as she approached but now the class all seemed to be working quietly. A scruffy boy sat at the teacher's desk in a jacket that was far too big for him.

"Good morning. My name is Miss Barker," she said. "Where is your teacher?"

# Dirty Bertie

"Yes, good morning," replied Bertie. "I am the teacher."

"Don't be ridiculous!" snapped Miss Barker. "Where is Mr Weakly?"

"Yes, Mr Weakly. That's my name," nodded Bertie, his glasses sliding down his nose. He pushed them back up again.

Miss Barker peered down at the boy. Teachers seemed to be getting younger and younger these days, but this was absurd. This one hardly looked any older than the rest of the class. When she'd first entered the room she could have sworn he had a finger up his nose.

"How old are you?" she demanded.

"Seven ... seventeen," said Bertie, correcting himself quickly.

"Seventeen? That's far too young to be a teacher!"

# Dirty Bertie

"Yes," said Bertie. "It is for a normal teacher but it's 'cos I'm more cleverer than normal."

"More cleverer?" repeated Miss Barker.

"Yes," said Bertie. "I used to get ten out of tens at school all the time. So in the end they said I just ought to get on and start teaching."

Miss Barker was about to reply but she was interrupted by a strange knocking sound.

"What's that noise?" she said.

"What noise?" asked Bertie.

"That banging noise."

"Oh that," said Bertie. "That's just Miss Todd, teaching next door. She gets a bit cross sometimes and she starts banging on the walls and things."

"Banging on the walls? Good heavens!" said Miss Barker.

She made a note in her black file and turned back to Bertie. "Well," she said, "if you really are Mr Weakly you better get on with the lesson."

"What?" said Bertie.

"The lesson. The lesson you're teaching."

"Oh yes, that," said Bertie. He gulped and pushed his glasses back up his nose. Miss Barker's face had gone all blurry. She seemed to be waiting for him to start. But what could he teach? He knew a lot about fleas – maybe he should draw some fleas on the board?

# Dirty Bertie

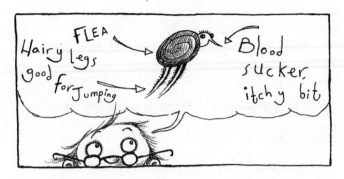

The banging from the store room started up again. He had to do something to drown out the noise.

"Maths!" he said, practically shouting. "We were just going to do a few sums." The class stared at him blankly, all except Darren who was pulling faces at him from the back row.

"Darren!" said Bertie.

"Yes?"

"Stand up," said Bertie.

Darren stood up.

"What is two plus two?" asked Bertie.

Darren thought a moment. "Four," he said.

"Very good, sit down," said Bertie. "Eugene."

"Yes, Bertie … I mean yes, sir," said Eugene, standing up.

"What are three twos, Eugene?"

"Six!" squeaked Eugene.

"Very good," said Bertie. "Nick."

Know-All Nick got to his feet. "Miss Barker—" he began, but Bertie cut him off.

"Pay attention, Nick. What is 2,740 times 7 million?"

Know-All Nick's mouth dropped open.

"Come on, come on," said Bertie, enjoying himself. "I haven't got all day!"

"I … I … don't know," stammered Know-All Nick.

# Dirty Bertie

Bertie peered over his glasses. "Tut tut, Nick! Extra homework for you tonight."

# CHAPTER 4

THUMP! THUMP! THUMP! The banging from the store room was deafening.

"Help!" cried Mr Weakly. "Can anyone hear me?"

Miss Barker stood up. "There's someone behind that door!" she said.

"No um ah … I don't think so," mumbled Bertie.

# Dirty Bertie

"Let me out! PLEASE!" begged Mr Weakly.

"There is someone in there," said Miss Barker. "I can hear them shouting!"

Bertie's heart sank. Miss Barker hurried over to the store room and spoke through the door.

"Hello?"

"Hello!" replied Mr Weakly. "Thank heavens! Who's that?"

"This is Miss Barker – the school inspector."

"Oh dear!" said Mr Weakly in a faint voice.

"What are you doing in there?"

"I'm locked in!" said Mr Weakly. "I came in to get a book and the door shut and now I'm locked in."

"Wait there!" said the inspector. "I'm going to fetch a teacher."

"I *am* a teacher," said Mr Weakly. "I'm Mr Weakly."

Miss Barker looked puzzled. "But I thought … Mr Weakly is right here…"

She turned back to the teacher's desk. But there was no sign of the scruffy boy she had been talking to – only a pair of glasses and a crumpled jacket that lay on his chair. Bertie had seized his chance to escape… He'd had enough of teaching for today. As he slid into his place he felt something sharp in his pocket. He pulled it out and stared at the silver key in surprise.

"Look!" he whispered to Darren. "It was in my other pocket all the time!"

# Dirty Bertie

Know-All Nick had turned round in his seat. He raised his hand in the air.

"Miss Barker! Miss Barker!" he said. "Bertie's got something to show you!"

The next day Miss Boot was back.

"Let's begin with Art," she said, with a gleam in her eye. "We'll need brushes and powder paints. Bertie, perhaps you'd like to fetch them from the store room?"

Bertie turned pale. He suddenly didn't feel well. "ME?" he said.

# Dirty Bertie

FIRE!

# CHAPTER 1

BOOF! Bertie landed two-footed in the big pile of leaves, scattering them everywhere.

"My go!" said Darren.

"HEY, YOU TWO! OFF THERE!" roared an angry voice. A bald, red-faced man was striding across the playground towards them.

# Dirty Bertie

"Uh-oh," said Darren. It was Mr Grouch, the school caretaker.

"What do you think you're doing?" demanded Mr Grouch.

"Um, jumping in leaves," said Bertie.

"Do you know how long it took me to sweep those up?" shouted Mr Grouch, waving his broom.

Bertie picked up a leaf and put it back on the pile. "Sorry Mr Grouch, we were only playing."

"Well DON'T play! Not where I'm working."

"But this is a playground."

Mr Grouch narrowed his eyes. "Are you trying to be funny?"

"No, Mr Grouch," replied Bertie.

"Then don't answer back. And keep out of my way!"

# Dirty Bertie

Mr Grouch glared after Bertie and Darren as they trudged off. Mr Grouch didn't like children and he didn't like mess. Most of all he didn't like Bertie. It was Bertie who left muddy footprints all over Mr Grouch's newly washed floors. It was Bertie who drew faces on Mr Grouch's spotless windows.

# Dirty Bertie

And Mr Grouch was sure it was
Bertie who had flooded the boys' toilets
by trying to flush away an entire toilet
roll. In Mr
Grouch's view,
Bertie was a
menace. In
Bertie's view,
Mr Grouch was a
vampire with a broom.

"What shall we do now?"
asked Darren, as they watched the
caretaker sweep the leaves back into a
neat pile. Bertie wasn't listening. He was
staring at something coming along the
road. A shiny red fire engine was slowing
down and signalling left. Bertie watched
with growing excitement as it turned in
through the school gates.

# Dirty Bertie

The fire engine halted in the car park
in front of the school and a woman in a
smart blue uniform climbed out. Bertie
and Darren hurried over.

"What's happening? Is the school on
fire?" asked Bertie,
hopefully.

"I'm afraid not," laughed the woman.
"I'm Val, what's your name?"

"Bertie. Are you a fireman?"

"Well I'm a fire fighter. We're here on

a visit. Didn't Miss Skinner tell you we were coming?"

Mr Grouch came storming over with a face like thunder. He pointed at the fire engine. "You can't leave that there! It's in my way."

Val smiled. "Sorry, Miss Skinner said to park it there."

"Did she now? We'll see about that!" said Mr Grouch, and he stormed off muttering to himself.

"Oh, dear," said Val, pulling a face. "Am I in trouble?"

"That's nothing," said Bertie. "You should try jumping in a pile of leaves."

## CHAPTER 2

Bertie could hardly believe it – a real fire crew! His school hardly ever got visitors. The last one they had was the nurse who checked them for head lice.

The fire crew stayed all morning and spoke to the whole school. Bertie learned how to dial 999 and what to do in case of a fire.

# Dirty Bertie

Outside Bertie and his friends
staggered around wearing helmets on
their heads. They sat in the red engine
and turned on the flashing blue light.
Finally they helped the fire crew unroll a
hose that stretched all the way across
the playground.

"Can we turn it on?" asked Bertie.

"Sorry, Bertie, not allowed," said Val.
"Only if there's a real fire."

Bertie wished he could help put out
a real fire. He imagined the school
crackling with flames and all the teachers
at the windows crying for help. He
would climb up the huge long ladder
and carry them down one by one.
(Miss Boot could wait till last. Come to
think of it, Miss Boot could climb down
by herself.)

# Dirty Bertie

# Dirty Bertie

At lunchtime, Bertie and his friends gazed across at the fire engine longingly. "I wish we could play on it," sighed Bertie.

"Miss Boot said we're not allowed," said Eugene.

"Well I think it's cruelty," said Bertie. "Leaving a fire engine right next to a playground and then telling us we're not allowed to play on it. It's cruelty to children."

Know-All Nick had sidled up to them unnoticed. "I bet none of you have ridden in a fire engine," he said. "I have!"

"When?" said Bertie.

"Hundreds of times," said Know-All Nick. "My uncle's a fireman and he lets me go in it whenever I like."

"I bet he doesn't," said Bertie. "How come we've never seen you?"

Know-All Nick shrugged. "Next time I'll ask him to drive right past your house, Bertie."

Bertie snorted. Know-All Nick was always making things up. Once he told them that he'd seen the Queen queuing at the bus stop. Bertie didn't believe that and he didn't believe Nick's uncle drove a fire engine. He probably drove a milk van.

"Anyway," said Bertie. "We don't want to go in your smelly old fire engine. We've got our own." He gripped an imaginary steering wheel and flicked an imaginary switch in front of him. "Come on!" he said.

# Dirty Bertie

"WOO! WOO! WOO!" went Bertie's siren as he drove off with Darren, Donna and Eugene hanging on behind him. Nick scowled, watching them go.

They drove the fire engine four times round the playground, stopping to put out several fires on the way. When they'd had enough they flopped down on the grass to rest.

"Oh no," groaned Darren. "He's back." Know-All Nick was running towards them, waving his arms excitedly.

"Quick!" he panted. "The school's on fire!"

"Yeah, very funny," said Bertie.

"I'm not joking," said Know-All Nick. "Look over there if you don't believe me!" He pointed to the far corner of the school. They all looked. Clouds of grey smoke rose into the sky above the roof of the hall.

"WOW!" said Bertie, getting to his feet. "It *is* on fire!"

Eugene stared open-mouthed. "What are we going to do?"

"Get the fire brigade!" said Donna. "I'll run to the staff room!"

"No!" said Know-All Nick, blocking her way. "They're not in there. I looked!"

"Then where are they?"

"I don't know!" said Nick. "Maybe they went out for sandwiches. But if we don't do something it'll be too late."

# Dirty Bertie

Bertie suddenly saw things clearly. For once, Nick was right. There was no time to search for the fire crew. The school was burning down and only he – Fire Fighter Bertie – could save it. Soon the flames would spread and in minutes the whole school would be ablaze. Trapped inside, the teachers would be burned to a frazzle. It was up to him.

"Come on!" he said.

"Where are we going?" said Darren.

"To put out the fire, of course!"

"But isn't that dangerous?" worried Eugene. "Shouldn't we fetch Miss Boot?"

"Miss Boot's no use," said Bertie. "This is a job for professionals."

Bertie reached the fire engine first. The clouds of smoke were billowing higher. He took command, shouting orders.

"Grab the hose! Now start pulling! Eugene, you get ready to turn it on."

"Okay!" nodded Eugene.

The orange hose began to unwind as Bertie, Darren and Donna dragged it towards the clouds of smoke. Other children came running to see what the noise was about. Eugene wished he had time to go to the toilet. Know-All Nick sat under a tree, watching them with a knowing smile.

At last they dragged the hose round the corner of the school. The smoke wasn't coming from the hall but from the yard behind it. Clouds of smoke stung Bertie's eyes, half blinding him.

"Now, Eugene!" he shouted. "Turn it on!"

# Dirty Bertie

The hose gurgled, coughed and sprang into life. A jet of water shot out with a tremendous whoosh. The hose wriggled like a snake, spraying water in every direction.

"Hold it still!" urged Bertie.

"We're trying!" said Donna. At last Bertie wrestled it under control and pointed it at the fire. With a hiss, the flames died down and fizzled out.

# Dirty Bertie

"We did it!" cried Bertie. "We saved the school." But as the smoke cleared he caught sight of Mr Grouch who had been knocked right off his feet by the first blast from the hose.

"Turn it off!" he gurgled.

Bertie stared in horror. His fire crew dropped the hose and ran. The school wasn't on fire at all. The only "fire" was Mr Grouch's bonfire, which was now a pile of damp, smoking leaves.

# Dirty Bertie

Mr Grouch sat in a puddle with water dripping from his soggy overalls.

"You wait, you little pest!" he growled. "You just wait!"

Bertie decided it was better not to wait. He turned and ran, with the angry caretaker squelching after him. He could hear Know-All Nick's shrill voice calling after him.

"Run Bertie, run! YOUR PANTS ARE ON FIRE!"

# CHAPTER 3

It was all Know-All Nick's fault, thought Bertie, as he swept up the soggy leaves. Nick had tricked him just to get him in trouble. But how was he to know the school wasn't on fire? You'd think teachers would be grateful when you tried to save their lives. You'd think they'd want to thank you.

But no – the way Miss Boot talked, anyone would think he'd tried to drown Mr Grouch on purpose! Well next time the school could just burn down.

"Can't I stop now?" he asked. "It's almost home time."

Mr Grouch looked at his watch. "Go on then. But don't think you're getting off lightly. Your parents will be hearing about this."

Bertie trudged home gloomily. Turning into Church Lane, he saw Pamela from his class. She was standing under a tree, gazing up at a tabby kitten clinging to one of the branches. It mewed pitifully.

"Poor thing!" said Pamela. "I've been calling her for ages.
I think she's scared."

# Dirty Bertie

"Oh," said Bertie. "D'you want me to get her down for you?"

He eyed the kitten sternly and spoke to it in his dog-training voice.

"Here girl! Down girl!" The kitten stared back at him without moving.

"I'll have to climb up," said Bertie.

Pamela looked up. "It's very high."

"Oh that's not high to me," said Bertie. "I've climbed hundreds of trees higher than that."

He took off his bag and jacket and caught hold of the lowest branch.

Luckily the tree was the kind that was made for climbing. Bertie wished there were more people to see his daring rescue.

# Dirty Bertie

As he climbed higher he pictured the kitten clinging gratefully to his chest. He could see her sitting on the end of a long branch. Bertie began to inch his way along, lying flat on his stomach.

"Have you got her?" called Pamela.

"Almost!" He reached out a hand. "Here puss! Here!"

The kitten got to its feet. But instead of going to Bertie, it yawned lazily and jumped down to the branch below.

In a few swift leaps and bounds it had reached the ground. Pamela scooped it up in her arms joyfully.

# Dirty Bertie

"It's okay, Bertie! I've got her!" she called. "She's all right!"

Looking down, Bertie suddenly felt *he* wasn't all right. The ground seemed a long way below – much further than he thought. In fact he wasn't sure how he was going to get down. His hands were sweating and he'd started to feel dizzy. He wrapped himself round the branch, not daring to move. Pamela's voice floated up to him.

"Bertie? What are you doing? You can come down now!"

"Um … I think you'd better call for help," said Bertie.

# CHAPTER 4

An hour later Bertie sat in the passenger seat of the fire engine.

"What road did you say?" asked Val.

"Digby Drive," said Bertie.

Val nodded. "I hope you're not planning to make a habit of this," she smiled, "because next time you'll be walking home!"

189

# Dirty Bertie

Bertie's rescue from the tree had caused quite a stir. A small crowd had gathered to watch when the fire engine arrived. A ladder was extended to Bertie with Val on top to help him down. When they were safe on the ground, everyone clapped and Bertie took a bow.

But the best part of all was that he got to ride home in the fire engine.

He looked out of the window. They were passing Cecil Road. Suddenly Bertie had a brilliant idea.

"Um, could we just turn down here?" he pointed. "It's sort of on the way, and there's someone I wanted to see."

# Dirty Bertie

Know-All Nick was in the lounge, watching his favourite cartoon on TV. WOOO! WOOO! WOOO! A deafening noise outside made him jump. He hurried over to the open window and looked out. He blinked. Was he dreaming?

A red fire engine was driving very slowly past his house with its lights flashing and its siren blaring. And sitting in the front seat, wearing a helmet and waving to him was Dirty Bertie. The siren stopped.

"Hi, Nick!" called Bertie. "Somebody called 999. They said to come to your house right away."

"My house?" said Nick. "Why?"

# Dirty Bertie

"BECAUSE YOUR PANTS ARE ON FIRE!" shouted Bertie.

# Dirty Bertie

# PANTS!

For Lynsey and Paul ~ D R

For Philip, old friendships are the best ~ A M

# Contents

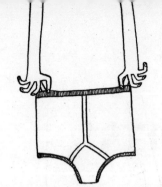

PANTS!

# CHAPTER 1

It was Thursday morning at the swimming pool. Bertie was getting changed after the lesson with Miss Crawl. His clothes lay scattered on the cubicle floor.

"HA! HA! I CAN SEE YOUR PANTS!" jeered a loud voice.

Bertie snatched up his towel. "Who said that?"

"BERTIE'S WEARING BLUE ONES!"
taunted the sing-song voice.

Bertie looked up. Two mocking eyes
leered at him over the cubicle wall. It
was his sworn enemy, Know-All Nick.

"Get lost!" said Bertie, throwing a sock
at him.

Nick stuck out his tongue. "Make me,
slowcoach!"

"Who are you calling a slowcoach?"
Bertie demanded.

"You. You're always last to get
changed," sneered Nick.

Bertie narrowed his eyes. "I bet I can
get changed a lot quicker than you."

"Oh yeah?" said Nick.

"Yeah!" said Bertie.

"All right," said Nick. "Let's have a race."

Bertie could never resist a race,

# Dirty Bertie

especially if it meant a chance to beat
big-headed Nick.

"Suits me," he said. "Last one back on
the coach has to sit next to Miss Boot."

Nick considered it. A smile spread
slowly across his smug face.

"I've got a better idea," he said. "Last
one on the coach has to come to school
tomorrow in their pants."

Bertie's jaw dropped.

# Dirty Bertie

"What's the matter, slowcoach, scared you're going to lose?" sneered Nick.

Bertie glared back. "Not a chance."

"OK, shake on it," said Nick. Bertie climbed on the bench and the two of them shook hands.

Bertie smiled. He would show that slimy slug who was slow. Nick wouldn't see him for dust. Wait till he told his friends about this: Know-All Nick coming to school in his pants – now that would be funny!

"Ready?" said Nick, through the wall. "Go!"

Bertie grabbed his trousers and yanked them on. His fingers wrestled with his shirt buttons. Socks next.

# Dirty Bertie

Where was his other sock? He wasted precious seconds hunting around the floor on his hands and knees. Who needed two socks anyway? One was plenty. He jammed on his shoes, his jumper, his coat. He stuffed his soggy trunks and towel into his bag and burst out of the cubicle.

"ARGH!" Bertie tripped over a mop and bucket that someone had left outside the door.

In seconds he was back on his feet and racing down the corridor. "Gangway!" he yelled, barging between Donna and Pamela. "Sorry! Emergency! Can't stop!"

Eugene flattened himself against the wall as Hurricane Bertie tore past. But turning the corner, a gigantic shadow fell across his path. "BERTIE!" thundered Miss Boot. "No running in the corridor!"

"But Miss, I—"

"Walk don't run, Bertie. WALK!"

Bertie groaned. He slowed to a walk as Miss Boot watched him like a hawk to the front door. Once outside, he flew down the steps, taking them three at a time. The coach was waiting in the car park. Almost there! Bertie dived through the door and flung himself into a seat.

"Yessss! I made it!" he panted. "I'm the

# Dirty Bertie

first one back!"

"What took you so long, slowcoach?" drawled a jeering voice. Bertie gasped. No, it couldn't be! It wasn't possible! Know-All Nick lounged on the back seat. His hair was combed, his tie perfectly knotted and he wasn't the slightest bit out of breath.

"Tough luck, Bertie, you lose!" He smirked. "I am *so* looking forward to you coming to school tomorrow."

# CHAPTER 2

Bertie sat in gloomy silence as the coach drove back to school. Darren pushed a bag of crisps under his nose. "Want one?"

Bertie shook his head.

"Are you ill?" asked Darren.

"Shhh!" said Bertie. "I'm trying to think."

"What about?" Darren munched his crisps noisily.

# Dirty Bertie

Bertie sighed. "If I tell you, you've got to promise you won't breathe a word."

Darren leaned closer. "OK."

Bertie looked around to check that no one could hear. He dropped his voice to a whisper. "I bet Nick I could beat him back to the coach after swimming."

"And?" said Darren.

"And I lost the bet. Now I've got to come to school tomorrow in my pants."

Darren grinned with delight. "In your pants? HA HA HA!"

"Shut up!" hissed Bertie.

"No … but seriously…" giggled Darren, "…in your pants? Hee hee!"

"Keep your voice down!" pleaded Bertie.

"I can't help it. That's so funny," chortled Darren.

# Dirty Bertie

Eugene turned round from the seat in front. "What's so funny?"

"Bertie's going to come to school in his pants," said Darren. "For a bet!"

Eugene stared at Bertie. "You're not?"

"No!" said Bertie, turning crimson. He was starting to wish he'd never mentioned it.

"But – in your pants?"

# Dirty Bertie

"Stop saying it!" cried Bertie. "You're meant to be my friends. You're meant to help me!"

Darren crunched another crisp. "It's not *our* fault," he said. "You made the bet. What can we do?"

Bertie thought about it.

"I know," he said. "Do it with me!"

"What?" said Darren.

"Come to school in your pants," said Bertie, desperately. "We'll all do it, together. It'll be brilliant! Why don't we?"

Darren and Eugene stared at him.

"You've got to be kidding!" said Darren. "There's no way anyone's going to see *my* pants."

"Eugene!" pleaded Bertie. "You'll do it, won't you?"

Eugene shook his head. "Sorry, Bertie.

# Dirty Bertie

I don't think my mum would let me."

Bertie slumped back in his seat and stared out the window, miserably. So much for friends. He was on his own.

Back in class, Bertie racked his brains. What was he going to do? Why oh why had he let Nick trick him into that stupid bet? He was certain that two-faced toad must have cheated. He was probably wearing half his clothes before the race even started.

In any case there was no going back now. A bet was a bet and he'd shaken on it. He tried to imagine walking into school wearing nothing but his pants. It didn't bear thinking about. People would be laughing at him for the next billion years.

# Dirty Bertie

No, he'd just have to think of some way out.

BRIIIING! The bell sounded for break. Bertie trudged out to the playground, lost in thought.

"Hee hee! There he is!"

Bertie turned round to see Angela Nicely and two of her little friends. Angela lived next door to Bertie. She was six years old and had been in love with Bertie ever since the time he gave her a sherbet lemon to stop her talking.

# Dirty Bertie

"What do you want?" glared Bertie.

"Hee hee! We want to … hee hee! … ask you something!" giggled Angela.

"Not now," said Bertie. "I'm busy!" He walked faster but Angela kept up with him.

"What colour are they, Bertie?" she simpered.

"Eh?" said Bertie.

"White or pink?" giggled Laura.

"Frilly or spotty?" sniggered Yasmin.

Bertie swung round to face them. "What are you talking about?"

"Your pants!" squealed Angela. "Nicholas told us. You're coming to school in your pants tomorrow!"

The girls burst into a fresh fit of giggles.

Bertie turned a deep shade of pink. "I … I'm not!" he stammered.

"Yes you are," said Angela. "Everybody says so."

"Listen! It's rubbish! I'm not!" said Bertie, desperately.

Angela edged closer to him, smiling sweetly. "I'm going to bring my camera, Bertie," she trilled. "I'm going to take a picture of you in your…"

Bertie didn't wait to hear any more. He turned and fled.

He hid in the cloakroom, till he was sure they had gone. This was worse than he'd ever imagined. Darren and Eugene knew. So did Angela and her friends. By now the news would be round the whole school. He should have guessed that big-mouth Nick would tell everyone. Tomorrow they'd all be waiting for him – whispering and sniggering.

# Dirty Bertie

If only he could think of some way out.
Bertie considered himself a master of
clever plots and cunning plans, but this
time his mind was blank. It was no use.
He wished he was a worm so he could
crawl into a hole and hide.

# CHAPTER 3

"BERTIE!" boomed Miss Skinner in assembly. "Out to the front, now!"

"Me, Miss?" said Bertie.

"Yes, you. And make it snappy, I haven't got all day!"

Bertie gulped and dragged himself out to the front. Why was everyone staring at him and sniggering?

# Dirty Bertie

"Haven't you forgotten something, Bertie?" said Miss Skinner.

Bertie looked down. He gasped. He was wearing nothing but his pants.

"ARGHHHHH!" he screamed – and woke up. He breathed a sigh of relief and sank back on his pillow. Thank goodness, it was only a nightmare. But wait – what was today? Friday! Pants Day! It wasn't a nightmare after all, it was really happening!

There was a knock on the door. Mum came in. "Aren't you up yet, Bertie? It's time for school."

"Urrrhh!" groaned Bertie. "I don't feel well. I think I've got Germy Measles."

Mum felt his head. "Hmm," she said. "I can't see any spots."

"I think they're invisible!" he mumbled.

"Don't be silly, Bertie. There's no such thing."

"How do you know?" said Bertie. "If they're invisible they could be all over me! I could be dying of them! I could—"

"Get dressed!" said Mum. "You're going to school."

Bertie flopped out of bed. He pulled out his drawer and looked inside. All of his pants were teeny-weeny. What he needed was extra-large pants to cover as much of him as possible. Wait a moment — his dad had lots of pairs of pants. Big pants. Surely he could borrow a pair?

Bertie tiptoed into his parents' room. He pulled open a drawer and dumped piles of pants on to the floor. Right at the bottom he found what he was looking for. A large pair of blue Y-fronts.

Bertie tried them on and looked in the mirror. They looked absurdly big, but they were the best he could find.

# Dirty Bertie

Mum and Suzy were eating breakfast in the kitchen. Bertie tried to sneak past them and reach his chair.

"HA! HA!" shrieked Suzy, catching sight of him.

"What?" said Bertie. "They're only pants."

Mum stared at him. "Good heavens, Bertie! Where are your clothes? And whose pants are those?"

"Dad's. I just need to borrow them!" said Bertie.

"Ha ha! Hee hee!" wheezed Suzy. "You should see yourself!"

"They're way too big," said Mum. "You've got plenty of pants of your own."

"Not like these. I need a really big pair!"

"Whatever for?"

"For a bet. I said I'd go to school in my pants!"

"Don't be ridiculous, Bertie. You can't possibly!" said Mum.

Bertie blinked. A wave of relief swept over him. Why hadn't he thought of it before? He had promised to go to school in his pants and he would.

"Never mind!" he laughed. "It's OK. Everything's OK!"

He danced out of the kitchen and back upstairs wearing the pants on his head.

# CHAPTER 4

Know-All Nick stood on the wall, keeping watch along the street. It was ten to nine and the playground was full to bursting. Everyone had come early to be sure of seeing Bertie's big moment. Angela Nicely had her camera at the ready. Darren, Donna and Eugene were arguing about whether Bertie would

actually go through with it. Darren said
yes. Donna said no. Eugene couldn't
make up his mind.

"Here he comes!" shouted Nick,
pointing up the road.

They all watched the entrance, eagerly.
Bertie rounded the corner and marched
in through the gates. Know-All Nick
stared in disbelief. Bertie was dressed as
normal in his jumper and jeans.

Nick jumped down from the wall and

marched up to him.

"We had a bet!" he fumed. "You cheated! You had to come to school in your pants!"

Bertie shrugged. "I have. I'm wearing them. Under my trousers."

"Wh … wh … what?" stammered Nick, turning pale.

"What's the matter, Nick?" asked Bertie. "Don't *you* wear pants under your trousers?"

"Of course I do," snapped Nick.

Bertie winked at Darren. "That's not what I heard. I heard you don't wear pants."

"No," grinned Darren. "None at all."

"I do!" protested Nick.

"I heard you went knickerless. Knickerless Nick," said Bertie.

"It's not true!" wailed Nick.

"But how do we know?" said Bertie.

"Because I say so!"

"You might be lying."

"I'M NOT!" yelled Nick. "LOOK!" He pulled down his trousers to prove it.

SNAP! went Angela's camera. Nick turned crimson. The whole school could see his pants and they were all laughing.

"I'll get you for this, Bertie!" he yelled.

FAME!

# CHAPTER 1

Bertie flung open the door and burst into the kitchen.

"I'd do anyfing for you, dear, anyfing! 'Cos you mean everyfing to meeeeee!" he sang in his gruff, droning voice.

Suzy groaned. Dad covered his ears.

"Lovely, Bertie," said Mum. "But maybe not quite so loud."

# Dirty Bertie

"Miss Boot says you should sing out," said Bertie. "I was singing out."

"We heard you," said Dad. He glanced at his watch. "We'd better go or we'll be late for the audition."

"Good luck, Bertie," said Mum. "Just do your best. And try not to cause any trouble."

Bertie trooped out to the car. He didn't see what trouble you could cause just by singing. He had been looking forward to the audition ever since he'd heard his parents talking about it. Bertie's dad belonged to the Pudsley Players and every year the Players put on a show at the local theatre. This year they were doing the musical, *Oliver!* Bertie had seen *Oliver!* on TV. It was about an orphan called Oliver who goes round

# Dirty Bertie

asking people for more and ends up rich.
When his dad said they were looking for
children to join the cast, Bertie had
jumped at the chance. He practised his
singing as they drove to the theatre.

"I'd do anyfing…" he droned.

"Bertie!" sighed Dad.

"What? I'm only singing."

"Well don't! You'll cause an accident.
And at least try to keep to the tune."

# Dirty Bertie

"I am keeping to the tune!" said Bertie. "That's how it goes… 'I'd do ANYFING…!'"

"BERTIE!" shouted Dad, gripping the steering wheel.

Bertie lapsed into silence. The trouble with some people, he thought, was they just didn't appreciate good singing.

At the theatre he found the dressing room crowded with eager children waiting to be called on stage. Bertie elbowed his way through the crowd and found an empty seat next to a pale boy wearing a large brown cap. It was only when the boy looked up and scowled that he recognized his old enemy, Know-All Nick.

# Dirty Bertie

"What are you doing here?" sneered Nick.

"What are *you* doing here?" replied Bertie.

"If you must know I'm going to be in the play," boasted Nick.

"Well so am I," said Bertie.

"Huh!" scoffed Nick. "They're not that desperate. Anyway, Miss Lavish only wants five boys. You don't stand a chance."

"Who's Miss Lavish?" asked Bertie.

"Don't you know? She's the director." Nick removed his cap and smoothed back his hair. "Anyway which part do you want?"

"The Artful Dodger," said Bertie.

Nick snorted. "Sorry, that part's taken. I'm going to be Dodger."

# Dirty Bertie

"Liar," said Bertie. "She hasn't even heard you sing yet."

Nick gave him a smug look. "That's what you think."

A woman with a clipboard poked her head around the door.

"Nicholas?" she said. "Miss Lavish is

ready for you now."

Know-All Nick pulled on his cap and went to the door. "Oh by the way, Bertie," he said. "Miss Lavish has heard me sing lots of times. She's my godmother." He stuck out his tongue and vanished through the door.

# CHAPTER 2

Bertie sat in the dressing room waiting
to be called. He would show that sneaky
slimeball, Nick. His audition would be so
good Miss Lavish would fall on her knees
and beg him to play the Artful Dodger.
The room started to empty slowly as,
one by one, the other children were
called on stage. An hour went by.

# Dirty Bertie

Bertie was the only one left in the dressing room.

"Bertie?" said the lady with the clipboard. "Miss Lavish will see you now. And please don't pick your nose." Bertie removed his finger. He bet the Artful Dodger picked his nose all the time.

Bertie stood in the middle of the stage and squinted into the spotlights. He'd never been on a stage before and he'd certainly never been asked to sing a solo. Miss Lavish sat a few rows back, scribbling notes. She was a large woman wrapped in a scarlet shawl. Bertie coughed nervously. Miss Lavish looked up.

"Hello dear. And you are?"

# Dirty Bertie

"Bertie," said Bertie.

"Lovely. And what are you going to sing for us?"

"Oh um … 'I'd do Anyfing'. It's from *Oliver!*" said Bertie.

# Dirty Bertie

"I know where it's from, dear," said Miss Lavish, peering over her glasses. She raised a plump finger. "Come in with the piano then."

Miss Plunk played the opening bars on the piano. Bertie turned and walked off stage.

"Where are you going now?" cried Miss Lavish. "Come back!"

"You said to come in with the piano," said Bertie. "I can't come in if I'm still here."

"I meant come in singing. Come in with the music!"

"Oh," said Bertie. He wished she'd say what she meant.

Miss Lavish nodded wearily at Miss Plunk. "Let's try again, shall we?"

The piano played. Bertie took a deep

breath and opened his mouth. To his horror he realized that the words had gone clean out of his head. He had practised them a million times but his mind was a total blank. He began anyway, hoping the words would come back to him.

# Dirty Bertie

"I'd um … anyfing … um … you …
um … anyfing! 'Cos you um … anyfing!
… um er …"

Miss Lavish's mouth had fallen open.
Whatever Bertie was singing it wasn't a
tune. She raised a hand to put a stop to
the awful dirge, but Bertie ploughed on,
bellowing any word he could remember.

# Dirty Bertie

"I'd … er … ANYFING! And you'd um … ANYFING!"

"Stop!" begged Miss Lavish, waving her hands. "Stop, stop, STOP!"

Bertie stopped. He waited for Miss Lavish to start clapping. True, he had missed out one or two of the words but no one could say he hadn't sung out. He bet no one else had sung out quite as well as he had. Miss Lavish took off her glasses.

"Thank you, Billy, that was ah … lovely. But I'm afraid I have all the children I need."

Bertie blinked. "Oh."

"But thank you so much for coming."

Bertie sniffed and wiped his nose. "You don't want me to be the Artful Dodger?" he asked.

# Dirty Bertie

Miss Lavish shook her head. "No, dear, we have our Dodger already."

Know-All Nick waved to Bertie from behind the stage curtain, with a 'told-you-so' smile on his face.

"I could sing something else," offered Bertie. "I know lots of songs."

"No, no more, please," said Miss Lavish hastily. "Run along now."

Bertie dug his hands in his pockets and trailed off.

Miss Lavish's assistant leaned over and whispered something in her ear.

"Wait one moment, dear!" she called. Bertie was back in an instant.

"I gather there is one very small part we have yet to cast," said Miss Lavish.

"Yes?" said Bertie.

"Well, what we really need is a dog."

# Dirty Bertie

"A dog?" said Bertie.

"Yes, the costume's rather small but you look about the right size. What do you think?"

"Me?" said Bertie. "Play a dog?"

"Yes. If you wouldn't mind?"

Mind? Bertie's eyes shone. It was a dream come true!

# CHAPTER 3

Mum was waiting for them when they got home.

"Well? How did it go?" she asked.

Bertie took off his coat. "Great. I got the part," he said.

"Really? They want you to be the Artful Dodger?"

"No, better than that. They want me

to be the dog," said Bertie.

"The dog?" Mum turned to Dad. "What dog?"

"It seems Mr Dodds needs a dog. He's playing Bill Sykes," explained Dad. "And they asked Bertie to do it."

"I get a costume and everything," said Bertie. "Miss Lavish says I ought to start practising right away." He padded past them on all fours and picked up Whiffer's bowl in his mouth. He dropped it at Mum's feet and began to whine.

# Dirty Bertie

Mum looked at Dad. "How many weeks do we have of this?"

"Ten," sighed Dad. "Look at it this way, at least he won't be singing."

Over the next ten weeks, Bertie went to rehearsals with his dad. His part turned out to be less exciting than he had hoped. Most of the time he had to trot after Mr Dodds or sit quietly while the other actors talked on and on. His big moment came in the final act when he dashed to the front of the stage and barked to bring the police running. Bertie practised that one "Woof!" a hundred different ways, but he couldn't help feeling his talents were going to waste.

# Dirty Bertie

In rehearsals he tried to add in a few 'doggy touches' to liven up the dull bits of the play. Whenever Know-All Nick came on stage, Bertie bared his teeth and growled fiercely. But Miss Lavish said his growling was drowning out the words and could he please keep quiet. Bertie took to scratching his ear with his paw. But Miss Lavish said he was 'destroying the atmosphere' and could he please keep still.

The following week, Bertie thought he could smell a cat and went sniffing

☆

around the stage. Miss Lavish lost her
temper and threw down her script.
Bertie sighed. He didn't see how he was
meant to play a dog that didn't growl,
scratch or even sniff. He might as well be
a goldfish! To make matters worse, there
was still no sign of his costume. Bertie
didn't have a chance to try it on until
the dress rehearsal. It was an itchy
brown suit. The head had floppy ears
attached and was three sizes too small.
Bertie complained to Miss Lavish but she
said she didn't have time for silly details.

# CHAPTER 4

Finally the big night arrived. There was a buzz of excitement as Mum and Suzy took their seats and the lights went down. The curtain drew back to reveal the painted streets of London Town.

Backstage, Bertie was still in the dressing room. "Hurry up! We're starting!" said Nick, pulling on his jacket.

# Dirty Bertie

"It's this head!" moaned Bertie. "It's got smaller. I can't get it on!"

"Oh give it here!" said Nick, impatiently. He grabbed the dog's head and jammed it down hard over Bertie.

"Mmmnff!" said Bertie in a muffled voice. "That's the wrong way round! I can't see!"

Nick wasn't listening. He had hurried out of the door, anxious not to miss his cue. Bertie tried to twist the dog head back round, but it was jammed on tight and wouldn't budge.

# Dirty Bertie

Mum and Suzy clapped as the first act came to an end

"Where's Bertie?" whispered Suzy. "I haven't seen him yet."

"Shhh!" replied Mum. "This is his big entrance."

Mr Dodds entered as Bill Sykes, making his way to Fagin's hideout. He looked round for his faithful dog, Bullseye, but there was no sign of him.

"Bertie!" he hissed. "Bertie!"

Backstage Dad looked round. "Where's Bertie? He should be on stage!"

At that moment, Bertie stumbled up the steps, still wrestling with his head.

"You're meant to be on," Dad hissed. He grabbed Bertie by the arm and

shoved him on stage. There were giggles
from the audience.

"What's he doing?" whispered Suzy.

"Oh dear," said Mum. "I think he's got
his head on back to front."

Mr Dodds took hold of Bullseye's
head and tried to twist it round. The
audience roared with laughter.

# Dirty Bertie

"Ow!" said Bertie loudly. "That hurts!"

Mr Dodds was sweating. "Shhh!" he muttered, thrusting Bertie behind a lamp-post where he couldn't do any harm. "Stay!" he commanded.

Sykes and Fagin started an argument but no one was paying much attention. They were all watching Bullseye. Bertie was rolling around on the ground, tugging at his head with both hands.

"Is this part of the story?" whispered Suzy.

"I'm not sure," replied Mum. "I don't remember it in the film."

Watching from the wings, Miss Lavish ground her teeth. At this rate Bertie would ruin everything!

"Miss Plunk!" she hissed. "Miss Plunk! Start the next song."

# Dirty Bertie

Miss Plunk thumped on the piano. Fagin sang "You've got to pick a pocket or two" and Dodger and his gang began to dance.

"Bertie! Get off!" urged Dad. Bertie trotted blindly in the wrong direction – straight towards the dancers who were whirling faster and faster.

Know-All Nick took a step back, tripped over Bertie, and tumbled straight into an apple cart. Apples spilled across the stage and under the dancers' feet. Miss Lavish watched in horror as Mr Dodds stumbled into a lamp-post and sent it crashing down on the streets of London. The tall scenery swayed dangerously.

"Look out!" shouted Dad. "It's going to fall!"

"Arghhhh!" screamed the actors,
running in all directions.

"What's happening?" asked
Bertie, left alone on stage.

CRASH! went the scenery
as it came tumbling down.

There was a hushed silence.
The audience waited to see if this
was the end of the show. Slowly
the dust cleared to reveal a
mound of broken scenery.

# Dirty Bertie

A door moved. From underneath it, Bertie scrambled out. He tugged at his dog's head and finally managed to pull it off. Puzzled, he looked around. *Where had everybody gone?* The audience were all staring at him in astonishment. Bertie suddenly remembered he hadn't given his one and only line.

# Dirty Bertie

"WOOF!" he barked.

The audience laughed and clapped and cheered. Bertie grinned and gave a low bow. He was still bowing when Dad brought the curtain down.

# Dirty Bertie

Turning round, he saw Miss Lavish, Mr Dodds and the rest of the cast advancing on him. Their hair was white with dust and their faces were grim.

"You wait," said Miss Lavish. "You just wait…"

But Bertie didn't wait. He did what any dog would do – he took to his heels and ran.

POOP!

AVAST THERE ME HEARTIES!

Come to Black-Eyed
Bertie's Pirate Party

Saturday 2 pm

Dress as a pirate

P.S. ‐ Bring me a present or
Walk ye Plank!

# CHAPTER 1

Bertie could hardly wait – he'd been
counting down the days to his birthday
for weeks and now it was almost here.
It was going to be the best party ever.
Bertie already had his pirate captain's
hat and plastic eyepatch. All he had
to do now was hand out invitations to
his friends.

# Dirty Bertie

"A pirate party? Great!" said Darren.
"When is it?"

"Saturday afternoon," said Bertie.

"Not this Saturday?"

"Yes!"

Darren's face fell. "But I'm going to
Royston's party!"

"Royston's?" Bertie couldn't believe his
ears. Royston Rich was the biggest show-
off in the school and no one in Bertie's
class liked him. "But you hate Royston!"

# Dirty Bertie

"I know but he's having a swimming party. He's got a pool in his garden with a wave machine and everything!"

"But what about my party?"

Darren shrugged. "Sorry, Bertie. Royston gave out his invitations last week. Didn't you get one?"

Bertie hadn't. Not that he cared. Who wanted to go Royston's rubbish party? He crossed Darren's name off his list. Still, if Darren let him down at least he could rely on Eugene...

"Saturday?" asked Eugene.

"Yes. You're coming, aren't you?"

Eugene turned pink. "I'd like to but I'm going to Royston's party."

"Not you as well!"

"Sorry, Bertie. He's got his own swimming pool with a—"

# Dirty Bertie

"I know! A wave machine and everything!" scowled Bertie.

"Yes and did he tell you about the inflatables? It's going to be brilliant. Everyone's going…" Eugene went pinker still. "Oh – aren't you, Bertie?"

"No!" snapped Bertie. "I'm having my own party and it'll be a billion times better than his."

Scratch! Bertie crossed Eugene off his list. At break-time he gave Donna her invitation. Scratch! She was going to Royston's party too. So was Alex, Dan, Stan, Sunil and Pamela. At the end of the day the only invitation left was for Angela Nicely. Bertie hadn't wanted to invite her in the first place – he'd only included Angela because he'd gone to her party. Scratch! Out went Angela.

# Dirty Bertie

That left – Bertie looked at his list –
no one at all. *Well, see if I care*, thought
Bertie. *I'll have a great party on my own.
Loads more cake and crisps for me!*
Hang on though, if no one came to his
party he wouldn't get any presents. And
playing pirates wasn't much fun when
the only enemy was Whiffer.

# CHAPTER 2

Bertie slammed the front door. He flung down his bag and clumped upstairs to his room. A minute later, Mum poked her head round the door.

"Bertie, are you all right? How was school today?"

"Terrible," grumbled Bertie. "No one's coming to my party."

# Dirty Bertie

"No one? Didn't you give out the invitations?"

Bertie explained about Royston Rich's swimming party.

"Oh dear!" said Mum. "Fancy it being on the same day as yours! Maybe we should move your party to next weekend?"

"That's years away!" moaned Bertie. "If anyone should move I don't see why it should be me. Why doesn't he move his smelly old party?"

His mum sighed. "Bertie, things don't always work out the way you want."

"Huh!" said Bertie, bitterly. "I bet if we had a swimming pool everyone would come to my party. Why can't we get a swimming pool in *our* garden?"

His mum gave him one of her looks and closed the door.

Bertie lay on his bed. It wasn't fair.
Who did Royston think he was pinching
all Bertie's friends? Just because he didn't
have any friends of his own! Well Black-
Eyed Bertie, the scourge of the seven
seas, wasn't beaten yet. If Royston was
boasting about his super swimming pool,
he would just have to think of something
better. He racked his brains. What did
pirates do when they weren't swabbing

decks or splicing the mainbrace?
Of course – they hunted for buried
treasure!

Bertie tiptoed into his parents' room.
He went straight to the present drawer
where his mum kept anything she didn't
want him to see. Inside he found party
hats, balloons – and a big bag of
chocolate coins. "Ahaar!" cried Bertie.
"Gold doubloons!"

# Dirty Bertie

Out in the garden he dug a hole and carefully slipped in the bag of coins. He was just smoothing over the earth when he heard a ring at the door.

It was Royston Rich.

"Oh hello, Bertie," said Royston, carelessly. "I brought your invitation."

Bertie stared in surprise. "You're inviting me?"

Royston shrugged. "Andrew can't come so I suppose you might as well. I couldn't think of anyone else."

"Well I can't come either, I'm having my own party," said Bertie.

"I know, but no one's going to yours, are they?" gloated Royston.

"Huh, that's what you think! Loads of people are coming."

"Yeah? Like who?"

"Like ... loads of people."

"Well everyone from our class is going to be at *my* party," boasted Royston. He pushed the invitation under Bertie's nose. "Keep it anyway, in case you change your mind."

Bertie snatched it off him. "I won't," he said.

"Suit yourself," said Royston. "You'll be missing the best party of the year. We're having a wave…"

# Dirty Bertie

SLAM! Bertie shut the door in his face.

He turned round to find Mum barring his way.

"Bertie, someone's been nosing in the present drawer."

"Oh. Have they?" said Bertie, innocently.

"Yes and a bag of chocolate coins is missing. I bought them as prizes for your party. Do you know anything about that?"

# Dirty Bertie

"Erm…" said Bertie.

"Bertie, if I find out you've eaten them…"

"I haven't!"

"Good, then you can give them back. Right now."

"But Mum, I need them for the treasure hunt! You can't have a pirate party without buried treasure."

Mum put a hand to her head. "Buried treasure? Bertie you haven't!"

"What?"

"Buried them?"

"Well I might have," said Bertie. "But it's OK, I know exactly where they are!"

"Where?" demanded Mum.

"Um … somewhere in the garden."

# CHAPTER 3

Saturday afternoon came. Bertie stood at the front room window staring along the road. He was dressed in his pirate hat and eyepatch. Whiffer, his faithful sea dog, sat at his side keeping watch.

It was half past two.

His mum came and joined him at the window. "I'm sorry, Bertie, I don't think

272

anyone's coming. Why don't you go to Royston's party? It's not too late."

"I don't want to!" glared Bertie.

"I'm sure you'll have fun," said Mum.

"I won't. I hate swimming!"

"Don't be silly, Bertie. All your friends will be there."

"Huh!" scowled Bertie. "I haven't got any friends."

Mum sighed. "Look, we'll have your party another day. Why don't you just go and enjoy yourself?"

"All right, all right!" said Bertie. "As long as Whiffer can come too."

Mum frowned. "It's a swimming party, Bertie, dogs aren't invited."

"Then I'm not going," said Bertie stubbornly. "If Whiffer can't go then I'm not going either."

# Dirty Bertie

Ten minutes later they arrived at
Royston's big house on Poshley Drive.
Bertie's mum buzzed the intercom at
the gates.

"Do come through!" sang Mrs Rich's
voice. "We're in the pool!"

The gates swung slowly open and
Bertie trudged through with Whiffer at
his heels. Screams and laughter came
from the enormous swimming pool in
the back garden.

"Hi Bertie!" waved Darren, zooming
down the slide and landing with a
splash.

Royston looked up. "Oh hello, Bertie!
I thought you were too busy to come?"

# Dirty Bertie

# Dirty Bertie

"I can't stay long," said Bertie, looking at his watch. "I've got people waiting."

"What do you think of my swimming pool? Super isn't it?"

Bertie shrugged. "It's all right."

"You better get changed. We're just about to start the wave machine!"

Bertie wandered over to the barbecue where Mr Rich was cooking hot dogs and enormous steaks. Whiffer's nose twitched at the smell of sausages.

"Hey!" shouted Mr Rich.

Bertie looked up. "Me?"

"Yes, you. Is that your dog?"

Bertie glanced down at Whiffer who was sniffing the meat. "He likes sausages."

"I don't care what he likes, take him somewhere else and tie him up. I don't want him near the food!"

# Dirty Bertie

Bertie dragged Whiffer away and tied him to a post on the lawn tennis court. "Sorry, Whiffer," said Bertie. "You stay there and I'll get you something to eat!"

Whiffer whined and pulled at his lead.

"Sit!" commanded Bertie. "Sit!" Whiffer sniffed around then squatted down on his hind legs. Uh-oh – that could only mean one thing. Bertie glanced around, hoping no one had noticed. It was lucky he'd remembered to bring along his pooperscooper just in case. He scooped the lump of poop into a small plastic bag. Now where to get rid of it?

# Dirty Bertie

He wandered back to the house, holding the bag at arm's length. By the pool he almost bumped into Mrs Rich carrying a tray of lemonade. Mrs Rich stopped and stared at the bag in Bertie's hand. She looked closer. Was that…? Good heavens! It was! She gasped.

"It's all right, it's only dog poo," said Bertie, holding the bag up for inspection.

"Ugh! Take it away!" cried Mrs Rich.

"I am taking it away," said Bertie. "But I'm looking for a bin."

"By the back door!" Mrs Rich flapped a hand. "Take it away before you drop it!"

Bertie walked on. He didn't see why Royston's mum was making such a big fuss. After all, dogs had to poo just like everyone else. And he'd been to a lot of trouble clearing it up – you would have thought she'd be grateful!

He was so busy grumbling to himself that he didn't notice the paper plate of raspberry jelly lying right in his path. Bertie stepped in the jelly and slipped. "Woaaaaaahhh!" He lost his balance and the bag slipped from his grasp. It sailed into the air and the lump of poop shot out like a torpedo.

# Dirty Bertie

Up, up, up it rose…

Then down, down, down – landing in the swimming pool with a loud PLOP!

"Uh-oh," said Bertie.

# CHAPTER 4

Royston zoomed down the slide, landing in the deep end with a great splash. He came up spluttering for air. What was that floating in the water? Something brown like a leaf.

"ARGGHHHH!" he shrieked.
"A POO! THERE'S A POO IN
THE POOL!"

Bertie had never dreamed one little piece of doggy-do could cause so much panic. Thirty children scrambled to get out of the pool, screaming as if a killer shark was after them.

"Do something!" cried Mrs Rich to her husband.

Mr Rich fetched a net and fished around in the deep end. But the poop had sunk to

the bottom and didn't want to be caught.

"Don't worry," said Royston. "My dad'll
sort it out. Then we can all go back in."

"Eeugh!" Donna pulled a face. "I'm not
going in there!"

"Nor me," said Pamela. "It's full of
pooey germs."

"It's yucky!"

"It's smelly!"

"But what about the party?" asked Eugene. "What are we going to do?"

Bertie pulled on his eyepatch and leaped on to a sunbed.

"Who wants to come back to my house for a pirate party?" he cried.

"Can we have sword fights?" asked Darren.

"Of course!" nodded Bertie. "And walking the plank. And a treasure hunt – with real chocolate coins!"

# Dirty Bertie

"Chocolate? Why didn't you say so before?" said Darren. "Come on!"

Thirty children charged out of the gates and down the road with Black-Eyed Bertie leading the way. It was going to be a brilliant birthday after all, he thought, and all thanks to Whiffer and his pongy present!

# Collect all the
# Dirty Bertie books!

# Look out for:

DAVID ROBERTS WRITTEN BY ALAN MACDONALD

Dirty Bertie

SNOW!